Thirteenth Child

Also by Karleen Bradford

Thirteenth Child

by

KARLEEN BRADFORD

HarperCollins*Publishers*Ltd

First published simultaneously in hardcover and trade paperback by HarperCollins Publishers Ltd: 1994
First HarperCollins mass market paperback edition: 1995

Canadian Cataloguing in Publication Data

Bradford, Karleen
  Thirteenth child

ISBN 0-00-647965-0 (mass market pbk.)

I. Title.

PS8553.R217T54 1994   jC813'.54   C94-931620-2
PZ7.B73Th 1995

---

95 96 97 98 99 ❖ OPM 10 9 8 7 6 5 4 3 2 1

Printed and bound in the United States

Thirteenth
Child

one

Stephanie took a step backward, then stopped. She looked behind her and gasped in terror. The cliff edge crumbled beneath her feet, and far below her the sea crashed against the jagged, pointed rocks in an insane fury.

"No!" she cried.

But the terrible form of her pursuer advanced remorselessly. His hands reached out for her throat . . . she could feel his hot breath burning her cheeks. . . . There was no escape!

"Kate! Wake up—it's your stop. You're home."

Kate came back to reality with a jolt and grabbed for her books. Flushing, she clambered over her seatmate, Barney.

"Plotting stories again?"

"No—" The answer was automatic, defensive, then she relaxed. "Well, yes. Sort of." She gave him a sheepish grin. It was just Barney, and he was about as close to a friend as she had. This was her second year at the high school that served all this area, but its size and the number of students who went there still intimidated her. She'd never made friends easily anyway; the only girl she'd been close to in public school had moved away. There were some kids here from her old school, but none who would ever look twice at her. Barney was the only one she'd become friendly with, and that only because he had happened to sit next to her on the bus a couple of times, and somehow or other it had developed into a habit. He was a year ahead of her, but he didn't seem to have any friends either.

A nerd, she thought. Just like me. But she liked him. He was comfortable to be with.

"See you tomorrow."

"See you," Barney answered.

Kate gained the aisle, then dropped a couple of books as she fought her way to the exit through outstretched feet and backpacks. As usual, she had loaded up at the library and was carrying far too much. She bit her lip as she bent to pick the books up, acutely conscious that the driver was waiting impatiently for her— she was the only one to get off at this stop, and Mrs. Murphy was running late. The noise was overwhelming. It was almost as if it were a physical weight in the air holding her down. She never got used to it.

As the bus pulled away, leaving her at the roadside, she stood for a moment looking at the building in front of her. Home. As always, it depressed her. A crummy gas station and snack bar, sitting all alone like an unwelcome wart on the side of a dusty Ontario highway. Painted in broad, garish, vertical orange and white stripes. As if it didn't stick out enough already. A stack of useless tires leaned against a drooping air hose that had stopped working months ago. A peeling, creaking sign in front of the snack bar read:

COFFEE
SNACKS
WORMS

Her eyes rested briefly on the burned-out remains of a house at one side of the station. There was nothing left but the foundation and a blackened, crumbling chimney. She ripped her gaze away from it, the old, familiar pain twisting inside. Why didn't her father get rid of it?

At the thought of her father, she looked around. He was nowhere in sight. Not a good sign. Her stomach knotted. She went around to the back of the service station and let herself into their kitchen. The screen door complained behind her and only closed halfway, letting in several flies.

"Close the *door*, Kate." Her mother, Angie, came in from the living room, voice a whine.

"All the holes in it, doesn't matter much whether it's closed or open," Kate answered, turning to face her.

Angie's face was set, as usual, in a mask of worried lines. She'd chewed all her lipstick off, and her hair hung in sad, brown wisps around her face.

I used to think she was pretty, Kate thought. I wonder when that stopped? Then she shrugged. Who am I kidding—I know when it stopped. The image of the burned-out house flashed behind her eyes like the black and white negative of a photograph.

"I have to go to the dentist," Angie went on. "This tooth is killing me. Can you take care of the snack bar for an hour or so by yourself? You'll have to do the gas too. Your dad. . . . " Her voice trailed off.

"Okay, Mom. Sure." Throwing her books down on the kitchen table, Kate hit the swinging door behind it with the flat of her hand so hard it bounced against the wall on the other side and came flapping back. It caught her on the shoulder. The pain was a relief, somehow. She went through into the snack bar.

She didn't have to ask where her father was. Up in the room above the garage. Resting. With a bottle of rye, "resting."

This was the day Burrell's delivered their groceries and stuff too. Angie had forgotten that. As usual. Kate dug underneath the counter for the order list.

There were only two customers, a man and a woman, both out-of-towners. They were drinking coffee, their plates pushed to one side. They seemed to be in the midst of a fight. The man shoved his chair back as Kate came toward them and handed her the bill and his money. Then they left, still arguing. Kate looked down at the amount scribbled on the bill and at the money. He'd left a fifteen-cent tip.

"Thanks a lot," she muttered, then set to clearing the table. She heard her mother crunch out over the gravel in the old pickup, but luckily no other cars drove in. She hated pumping gas. Usually managed to spill some of it on her hands, and the smell of it sickened her for hours afterwards. The air conditioner whined but didn't seem to do much good. Record heat for this early in the season, the TV had said. Kate wiped the sweat from her forehead; her blouse was plastered to her back.

A trucker came in and asked for coffee. He wasn't one of the regulars. She gave it to him, hardly noticing what she was doing. A scruffy kid came in—one of the Davidsons, who were camping in the trailer park down at the end of the lake, she thought, although there were so many kids running around, and they all looked so uniformly grubby, it was hard to tell them apart. He asked for worms. Not bothering to hide the disgust on her face, she went over to the worm refrigerator and took out a styrofoam tub containing peat moss and twelve worms. The kid and the trucker both left. She was alone again. Absent-mindedly, she took up the dish-cloth and began wiping the counter . . . .

Stephanie pressed herself against the wall, straining against the ropes that tied her fast. The tunnel was pitch-dark. Already she could feel the vibrations of the approaching train, hear its lonesome, wailing whistle. But, strain as she might, she knew it was hopeless. There wasn't enough clearance between the wall and the train for a living, breathing body! Frantically she twisted her hands, feeling the coarse rope cut into her flesh. She reached down to her shoulder and grabbed between her teeth the rope that bound her there. She ground her jaws together desperately . . . .

"I've got a knife! Give me all the money in the cash register."

Kate hadn't even heard the door open. She looked up. A thin, sick-looking boy was leaning toward her. Dark hair hung down over his eyes in lank strands; his forehead was beaded with sweat.

A knife? It occurred to Kate that Stephanie had never been threatened with a knife. The time might come when she would be, and Kate didn't know anything about knives.

"What kind of knife?" she asked.

"What do you care what kind of knife?" the boy demanded. "It's a sharp knife, okay? You don't want to find out how sharp."

With a shock, Kate came back to reality. Then she took a closer look at him. Both of his hands were on the counter and there was no sign of a knife anywhere.

He doesn't look all that much older than I am, she thought. And he looks scared silly. I'll bet he doesn't have a knife. The boy seemed to sag forward for a moment, and put a hand up to his forehead as if suddenly dizzy. No way does he have a knife, Kate decided.

"Why?" she asked.

"Why what? Look—" He straightened up and glared at her. His face was white.

On drugs? Kate was suddenly more concerned. That was something else. She snuck a look at the clock—the Burrell's man wasn't due for another half-hour at least. Then she looked back at the boy. His eyes looked all right. She'd seen a trucker once who was freaked out on drugs. This guy didn't look anything like that. And even kids at school—you could usually tell. He was just sick. That was it.

"Are you going to get that money or am I going to have to cut you?" The words were threatening, but they wavered and he still made no move toward a weapon. Kate made up her mind.

"Why do you want money?"

"Why?" he echoed, his voice desperate.

"Because I'm hungry, that's why. I haven't eaten in two days."

"Well, that's not too bright," she said, throwing the dishcloth back into the sink. The boy's mouth dropped open. A slightly confused look took over from the glare.

"What I mean is, if you're really starving and you steal money from here, that's not going to help you much. You can't eat money, can you?"

He started to say something, but the words seemed to stick.

"Once you get the money," Kate went on, "you're going to have to take off fast, right? Then I'll call the police. Then, as far as I can see, they'll either catch up with you and drag you into the police station—and you can be sure they won't feed you there—or if you do get away you'll have to hitchhike or something and get as far from here as you can, as fast as you can. Either way, you're not going to get anything to eat, and you're still going to be hungry." As she spoke, Kate turned to the back counter and began slapping margarine onto slices of bread.

"What are you doing?" The belligerence was rapidly deteriorating into bluster.

"Making you a sandwich, of course." She added a couple of slices of ham and some lettuce, tossed it onto a plate, cut it, and pushed it over to him.

He stared at it, then back at her.

"Go ahead, eat it."

He hesitated for a moment, poised as if ready to run or attack, but even he didn't know which. Then, as if of its own accord, his hand reached for the sandwich. It was gone in four bites.

"You weren't kidding, were you?" Kate asked. She made another one. She set this in front of him, then filled up a mug with milk.

The boy didn't say a word, just sank onto a stool and wolfed the second sandwich down even more quickly than the first. Kate cut off a generous slice of apple pie and slid that in front of him as well.

When he finished, he pushed himself back from the counter and looked up with slightly glazed eyes.

"You work here all the time?" he asked.

"My dad owns the place," she answered shortly.

"He let you give away food like this?"

"No."

Times were even harder than usual lately and Kate knew that every bit of food was counted and measured. Somehow or other, her dad always seemed to be sober enough to see to that. She'd answer for this.

The boy stared at her in wary silence. Kate was beginning to feel uncomfortable. What was she going to do now?

"You ever done anything like this before?" she asked finally, gesturing toward the cash register. "I mean, you know, tried to hold up a place?"

He looked away, uneasy. "No."

"Just as well," Kate said. "You're not too good at it."

"Guess not." He ran a hand through his hair and tossed it back out of his eyes, face still averted.

There was another awkward silence. Kate gathered up the mug and plates and began to wash them.

"What were you planning on doing? After you left here?" She concentrated hard on scrubbing.

"Hitching a ride west. Going to try and find a job."

"I don't think you'll find much out there. Things are just about as bad there as around here, they say. My dad knows a guy—he went out a few months ago. Couldn't get any kind of a job and had to hitch his way back. Got home a week ago, tired, broke, and sick as a dog."

The boy stood up. The food seemed to have revived him and the color was coming back to his face, but he was still wary, still defiant.

"I haven't been able to find anything—what am I supposed to do?"

Kate abandoned the dishes. "You know anything about boats?" she asked.

"Boats! I should think so. Been brought up around them all my life. Don't really know anything but boats."

"And motors?"

"Sure. You know boats, you know motors."

"Seems to me," Kate said, "that a person who

doesn't know about anything except boats shouldn't be heading to the prairies, of all places."

Suddenly, the boy relaxed. He looked straight at Kate, grinned, and his whole face changed. "You've got a point," he said.

Kate felt a weird kind of flip inside her chest. It took her by surprise. When he grinned like that— he was really kind of good-looking. . . . She spoke quickly, trying to cover up her confusion.

"Old Jed, up near town," she said, "he was in the other day. He's starting to get his boats ready for the tourist season and he was saying he needs someone to help him."

"You think he might hire me?"

"Don't see why not."

"A guy who tried to hold you up?"

"He doesn't need to know that." Kate turned away and started back in at the dishes. "His place is down by the river, just before you get into town. There's a big sign there: 'Jed's Boats for Hire.' You can't miss it." She began to stack the dishes in the drainer. Then she picked up the dishcloth out of the sink and started to wipe the counter again with it, rubbing hard at a burn mark that had been there for as long as she could remember. "We need worms too. The guy who supplies us left town last week. You know how to pick worms?"

"Sure. Who doesn't?"

Who doesn't, indeed, Kate thought, nose wrinkling.

"Anyway," she went on, "there's work around here if you want it, I guess." She wiped her way down to the other end of the counter, her back to him.

"You wouldn't say anything?"

"No. Why should I?"

"I can think of a lot of reasons why."

"Forget it. You didn't mean it. I never believed you, anyway."

He turned to head for the door, then stopped to stare back at her for a moment. There was a strange look on his face. "You really should be more careful, you know," he said.

Kate stared after him.

The Burrell's truck pulled in soon after, Rob at the wheel. Rob was one of Kate's favorites among the drivers. He always had a new joke and could usually josh her out of the blackest mood, but right now she was distracted. She flipped a grilled cheese sandwich onto a plate, threw a burger together, and poured coffee for two men at the corner table, then grabbed for the delivery invoice. Her mind still echoed with the boy's words.

"You should be more careful," he had said.

Was it a warning?

"Not quite with it today, are you, Kate?" Rob teased, as she ticked off the wrong item on her list for the third time.

"I'm tired." The words came out with more of a snap than she'd intended.

"Hey! What's with you?" Rob took a closer look at her, but Kate bent her head over the list and wouldn't look back at him. "Anything wrong, Kate? Anything happen?"

Kate just shrugged, then the door opened and a group of late-afternoon regulars streamed in, all talking at once. She turned quickly to them.

"Hot enough for you, Kate?" Bob Dowles from the local hardware store called out.

"Iced coffee, Kate, quick before I melt," Norris Lamont, the druggist, put in. He staggered a bit, wiped his brow with an exaggerated swipe, and sank into a chair at one of the tables. Bob and the other two men pulled out chairs and joined him.

"Cokes for us, Kate," Jimmy Bent added. He and his son, the fourth member of the group, ran a sporting-goods store in town. The four men often dropped in afternoons for a drink before heading home.

"Your dad around, Kate? Didn't see him out front," Jimmy Bent asked.

"He's . . . not here right now."

"Kind of busy for you all by yourself, isn't it?"

They exchanged glances; Jimmy Bent raised an eyebrow.

"I can manage," Kate answered. "Just check off the rest of the stuff yourself, Rob, will you? Seem to think you can do it better than me, anyway."

She'd seen the look that had passed between the men. They had used to be her father's best friends. Main reason why they'd begun coming in here in the first place. She busied herself with the coffee and Cokes.

That guy. He hadn't had a knife. He'd just been bluffing. She was sure of it.

Wasn't she?

two

Kate downed a glass of milk, praying the school bus would get there before her father appeared. No luck. Just as she was finishing, he walked into the kitchen from the garage where, presumably, he had spent the night. He'd come through the snack bar, and from the stormy look on his face she was sure he'd done a quick inventory.

Angie jumped up and headed for the stove.

"Coffee, Steve?" Pretending as usual there was nothing wrong, her voice artificially bright.

"Yeah." He sat down heavily at the table and let his head drop into his hands.

Kate looked at him. Suddenly memories of how it used to be came flooding back. Movies on a Saturday afternoon with him, and ice-cream cones afterwards. Curled up in the big chair in the living room, on his lap, with the wonderful, shaggy smell of him, and the feel of his arm around her. She'd felt so safe then. He had been so strong. She'd been so sure he could protect her from anything. And things were going to be so great. He had it all planned out. He used to sit her mom and her down in the evenings and describe how it was going to be . . . .

He glared up at her and the memories vanished. She tensed, not sure of what was coming next.

"Lot of food used up yesterday and not much money in the till." Steve rubbed at his forehead and winced, as if with pain. "Either of you know anything about that?"

"I. . . . " How to explain? "I gave some to a friend. You can take it out of my pay."

Her pay. That was a laugh. Her father paid her the bare minimum he could get away with. At the same time he wouldn't even discuss letting her work at the mall on Saturdays or evenings. Said it was her duty to help out here.

"How many times have I told you—" Steve began.

Mercifully, the school bus beeped outside. Kate scooped up her books and headed for the door.

"Kate," her mother said, but she slammed on out, pretending she hadn't heard.

It wasn't until the bus pulled away that she realized she'd forgotten the lunch she'd made the night before and left in the refrigerator. That was probably what her mother had been trying to tell her. A flash of guilt swept through her. It wasn't Angie's fault she couldn't cope with things—she'd never been asked to in the old days. Steve had called her his "baby doll" and spoiled her rotten. She just didn't know what to do now. Still, the way she crept around worried and half scared to death all the time, but trying to make out nothing was wrong, drove Kate wild. It sure didn't help matters.

Barney tried to make conversation, but she answered him in monosyllables and finally he gave up.

"One of those days, eh?" he said.

"Yeah," Kate answered, staring out at the fields as they flashed by, parched and dry-looking in the heat. For a moment she was tempted to let go and pour everything out.

"I know how it feels."

There was something in his voice. Something grim. It didn't sound like Barney at all. Then he whipped around in his seat, his face suddenly excited.

"There's the bike, Kate! The one I was telling you about." He pointed outside. "It's used, but in fantastic condition, and dirt cheap. A 1982 Honda Nighthawk 400. And only seven hundred dollars. Isn't that unbelievable? It is so cool, Kate."

Kate looked, but all she had time to catch a glimpse of was a group of bikers in ripped T-shirts and helmets lounging around the storefront of a motorcycle dealership that had just set up there. Some of them even had leather jackets on in spite of the heat. Must be sweltering, she thought.

"Great. All we need around here. A bunch of Hell's Angels creeps."

"They're not Hell's Angels. They're the Black Widow Riders." Barney flushed as she turned to stare at him.

"How do you know that?" she asked.

"Well . . . I met them, sort of. Some of them, anyway. When I went to look at the bike. And they're not creeps. They're perfectly normal—almost."

Kate's eyebrows shot up.

"They're okay, really they are," Barney insisted. "Bikers get a bad rap."

The impulse to confide in Barney died. He wouldn't be interested in her problems. Besides, this was family business. It wouldn't be right to talk about it.

English was third period. Usually it was Kate's favorite class, but today she couldn't concentrate. Her dad was getting worse and worse. Two nights ago, after she had gone to bed, she had heard him ranting even louder than usual— suddenly there had been a loud thump. Her mother had cried out, then there was silence. The next day Angie's eyes were swollen from crying. Nothing unusual about that, but there was a bruise on her cheek.

"Walked into the cupboard door," she had mumbled quickly when she saw Kate staring at it.

Could he . . . ? Could he actually have hit her? He'd never gone that far before, although, when Kate was smaller, even when things had been going well for them, he'd given Kate some terrible spankings. He'd always had a violent temper. That was the whole reason . . . .

"There were some good stories, some not-so-good stories, and some that seemed copied out of a *True Confessions* magazine. Kate, we'll start with yours."

Kate's head snapped up. Hers? Her story? Surely Mr. Evans wasn't going to read it aloud!

"The sun beat down on the blinding white sands of the beach. Palm trees swayed in the slight ocean breeze. People lounged on deck chairs, swirling cold drinks casually in their hands. It looked like an ad for paradise, but Stephanie knew the evil that lurked behind the scenes. She knew the terror that stalked this same beach when the full moon replaced the blazing sun, and the sands chilled ominously . . . .

"Kate, when was the last time you 'lounged on a tropical beach,' let alone with a 'cold drink swirling in your hand'?"

Kate grew very still and started to shrivel up inside. She kept her face so expressionless it felt like a mask.

"You really can write well, Kate," Mr. Evans went on, ignoring the giggles coming from various parts of the room, "but how often have I told you—told all of you," he said, addressing the whole room now, "write about what you know!"

Kate stared straight ahead, willing herself to block out Mr. Evans, the whole class, everything around her. Write about what she knew? Selling worms and pumping gas. That was what she knew. Day after day after day. Write about that? Sure.

A few days later, when she pushed through into the snack bar after school to start work, there were more people than usual there. The room was noisy with an unaccustomed buzz of conversation.

"Kate, did you hear?" The Davidson kid was back, his eyes wide with excitement.

"Hear what?"

Angie was frantically washing cups, and she motioned Kate toward the table where the usual group of men were talking.

"See if they want more coffee, Kate," she hissed.

"The drugstore was robbed!" he said, his voice shrill. "Wasn't it, Mr. Lamont?"

"Sure was," the druggist answered. "Last night. Just as Ned was closing up. Guy came in, ski mask over his face, and threatened him with a knife. Got near a hundred dollars—luckily I'd taken most of the money to the bank when I left—then got clear away. Police are out all over looking for him."

"Any idea who did it?" The Davidson boy seemed about to burst with awe.

"Nope. Ned said he couldn't recognize the

voice. Said the guy sounded young, though."

"Probably just some punk passing through," Bob Dowles put in. "Probably miles away by now. Bring us some more of that great coffee of yours, Kate, will you?"

"You never know," Jimmy Bent said. "Lot of new people around town. Kind of people we never had here before. I don't like it much, myself."

Kate apologized as she spilled the coffee on the table. She mopped it up quickly with shaking hands. A coincidence? It had to be. That guy hadn't gone through with the robbery here. He probably had a job by now—he wouldn't have tried another hold-up so soon, and in the same town . . . .

The snack bar didn't usually close until ten, but by nine there was no one there. Kate sat behind the counter, staring at the homework spread out in front of her. Her mind was not on math, however; it was whirling in confusion. When the door opened, she looked up, startled.

The boy walked in.

Her heart took a painful leap and she let out a gasp before she could stop herself.

He came up to the counter. He seemed to loom over her—taller than she'd remembered. She caught her breath, tried to speak, but the words wouldn't come out.

"What's the matter? Did I scare you? Sorry." He looked around. "You always stay here alone at night? Not too safe, that, is it?"

"My dad," Kate finally managed to get out.

"He's in back. . . . " A lie. Her father was out and Angie was in their living room, television blaring so loudly she wouldn't have heard a bomb go off.

The boy shrugged.

"I got that job with Jed." He leaned up against the cash register. One hand reached out casually to play with the keys. "Got some money now."

Kate went rigid. He reached into his pocket and pulled out a few bills.

"How much do I owe you for the food the other day?"

"It's okay. You don't have to . . . ."

"Sure I do. I want to. Anyway, money's no problem now. Ten dollars okay?"

"That's too much . . . ."

"Well, you need a tip, don't you? And taxes and all. Take it. I mean it. Money's going to be okay now."

Woodenly, Kate allowed him to press the bill into her hand.

"Came by to pay that and to see about the worms."

"Worms?"

"Yeah. Remember? You said you needed someone to pick worms."

"Oh. Yes. Worms." Kate forced herself to move toward the door to the back room. "I'll just get the stuff."

The boy followed her through before she could stop him. In the kitchen, he looked around. "This is nice—kind of cosy."

The television thundered on in the living room.

"Cosy!" In spite of her fear, Kate looked at him incredulously. What kind of a home had he come from if he found this bare, linoleum-floored kitchen cosy? The paint was peeling from the walls and there was a huge damp spot on one corner of the ceiling.

"Yeah. Kitchen at home was so deep in dirty dishes all the time you couldn't even see it. Tried to clean it up now and then, but with my mom and her boyfriends. . . . Never lasted too long." He shrugged again. "Anyway. Where's the worm gear?"

"I'll get it." Kate fumbled with the handle of a cupboard door, hands sweaty, then managed to pull it open. She knelt to rummage on the floor at the bottom, acutely conscious of him standing behind her. She pulled out two cans with Velcro tapes attached to them: one to be strapped on the left leg, to hold the worms, and one for the right leg, to hold the rosin to keep your fingers from getting too sticky. The worm can was slimy and smelled. She picked it up with the tips of her fingers. Where was the headband with the light on it? There it was, thrown down under all the rest of the stuff. She hoped the battery hadn't run out. She tested it, still kneeling half inside the closet, and willed her heart to stop pounding. She backed out and handed all the gear to him.

"You going out tonight?" The words were forced—strained. The boy didn't seem to notice.

"Sure. I'll bring the worms in tomorrow, in

the morning, early. That okay?" But he made no move to go. He looked toward the living-room door thoughtfully.

Trying not to be obvious about it, Kate moved toward the drawer where the knives were kept. There was a good big butcher knife in there . . . .

Idiot, she told herself. As if you could really use it. This isn't a Stephanie story, this is for real.

He finally turned to go. Kate let out a deep breath, then tensed again as he stopped and pivoted back toward her.

"By the way," he said. "My name's Mike. Mike Bridges." He paused. "What's yours?" he asked, when Kate didn't speak.

"Kate Halston."

"Nice name. You get in trouble about that food the other day?"

"No more than usual," Kate answered. With an effort, she made her voice sound casual. "I leave for school about eight. Can you bring the worms before then?"

"Sure. No problem. See you." He turned again and this time did leave.

Kate heard the outside door slam. Like a spring suddenly released, she raced through, locked it, and reversed the OPEN sign. Ten o'clock or not, this place was closed. She stood for a moment, willing her breathing to get back to normal and her heart to slow down, then she went back and gathered up her homework; there was no way she could concentrate on it now. She'd get up early and finish it in the morning.

Would she have used the butcher knife? If he *was* the guy who had held up the drugstore, and if he *had* gone for her in the kitchen—would she have had the courage? Stephanie wouldn't have hesitated for a moment. If he had made a grab for her and she had picked up the knife and plunged it into him, then what? Would he have fallen down and died right away, or would he have had time to strangle her first? In books people collapsed as soon as they were stabbed, but if she had missed everything vital and just wounded him . . . ?

And if she did kill him—would the police believe it was in self-defense? That he'd threatened her before? They'd ask why she hadn't reported it. She could see it now—in jail with prostitutes, with murderers. Other murderers, she reminded herself. She would be one of them. If no one believed her—how old would she be before they let her out? She could just see herself, gaunt and hollow-cheeked, thirty years old at least, emerging from the doors of a dark and forbidding prison.

The gates clanged shut behind her. There wasn't a soul to greet her. Her parents had both died while she was locked up. No one else cared. A life ruined . . . . A future of despair . . . .

She turned off the snack-bar lights, went through into the back, and climbed the stairs to her room. The television yammered on. She dumped the usual pile of books on her bed off onto the floor and lay down, fully clothed, her mind running around like a hamster in an exercise wheel.

three

Mike turned up the next morning at a quarter to eight, bucket of worms in hand. Kate saw him through the screen door just before he knocked.

"Who the hell's that, this early in the morning?" her father growled.

"It's a boy I hired to pick worms for us, Dad," Kate answered. "Johnny quit. Remember?"

"Johnny quit? When? I don't recall that." For a moment Steve seemed confused. He looked, mouth slightly open and eyes vacant, first at her and then at Mike standing in the doorway. He hadn't shaved or combed his hair, and his flannelette shirt, too heavy by far in this heat, was dirty and buttoned crookedly. Kate felt embarrassment wash over her as she saw Mike looking at him.

"Got a bucketful," Mike said. His voice was offhand, but his eyes were wary.

"How much you paying this kid?" The confusion was gone, the belligerence back.

Kate could see Mike begin to bristle.

"Now, Steve," Angie began.

"Shut your mouth, Angie. This here is business between Kate and me. None of yours."

Kate winced. "Same as what we paid Johnny, Dad." She turned quickly to Mike. "Here, I'll show you where to go," she said, hustling him out the back door.

"Your dad always that grouchy in the mornings?" Mike asked as they made their way toward the back of the garage, where the empty worm tubs were stacked.

Anger flared. Kate felt her ears burn red. "That's none of your business!" she snapped.

"Sorry." He didn't sound particularly apologetic.

"I suppose your dad is a model of politeness." Kate's words dripped sarcasm.

"Got no dad. Leastways none that I know of. Asked my mom once and she told me *that* was none of my business." Mike's voice was controlled, carefully casual.

Now Kate's whole face flamed. She grabbed up several worm tubs. "Put a dozen worms in each." The words came out sharp and bossy.

"Yes, ma'am!" Mike grinned, making a joke of it, but his eyes had gone hard and bright.

A shiver ran through Kate. She crossed her arms protectively over her chest and watched as he filled the tubs, making no move to help.

When he finished, they carried them back to the snack bar. Without thinking, Kate made for the cash register and clanged the drawer open. Her heart took a leap as she saw the drawer was stuffed with bills. Her father must have forgotten to empty it the night before, and yesterday had been busy. Mike's eyes widened briefly when he saw them, then his face went blank.

"Kate?" Her father's voice roared out from the kitchen. For once she was grateful for it.

"In a minute, Dad." She started to count out Mike's money.

"What's with the junkpile next door?" Mike asked as he pocketed it. "Have a fire?"

Kate slammed the drawer shut hard enough to knock a stand of mints off the counter beside it onto the floor.

"You really do like to poke your nose in where it's none of your business, don't you?"

"Just making conversation," Mike answered easily. "By the way, upside down is best."

"What?"

"Upside down. The worm tubs. Stack them upside down. The worms always head for the bottom, so then when you turn them right side up again and open them for your customers to check, they'll all be up at the top, lively and wriggling. Be better if you charged for a dozen and put in thirteen too. Customers like that. Makes them think they're getting something for nothing."

Kate's eyebrows quirked up. Another sarcastic comment was on the tip of her tongue, then she thought better of it. In spite of the casual tone of his voice, Mike's eyes were still anything but friendly. She started turning the tubs over.

"When do you think you'll need more?"

"Depends how fast we sell these. Fishing's been pretty good lately—maybe in a couple of nights."

"Kate! Get in here! I want to talk to you before you go off to school!"

Mike headed for the door. "Okay. See you then."

Kate looked after him, ignoring her father for the moment. Steve was probably just going to bug her about the worms, anyway. The sun was blazing down, even this early. The snack bar was already stifling, and she could see the heat shimmering in waves off the tarmac outside. There didn't seem to be a breath of wind. It was a long hike into town. Maybe Mike would get lucky and hitch a ride. She wondered where he was staying. She wondered where he'd got the money to pay her back last night.

Jed might have paid him in advance, she thought. He could have. Not like him, though. She rubbed at her arms, shivery again in spite of the heat. Maybe she was making a big mistake. Maybe she was being the world's biggest fool.

The school bus honked and she jumped. At least she wouldn't have to argue with her father about the worm money. She made a dash for her books.

"Did you hear the radio this morning?" Barney asked, as soon as she had settled herself down into her seat. He seemed upset about something.

"Not really," she answered. "Why?"

"There was more stuff about that guy who ripped off the drugstore. You didn't hear it?"

"No." Kate forced herself to sound bored, as if she couldn't care less, but her heart started to pound. She braced herself for whatever Barney was about to say next, but he fell silent. She looked sideways at him. He was biting his lip and looking out the window.

What's with him? Kate thought. Just then Melanie Davis poked her head around from the seat behind them.

"He's left-handed! He held the knife in his left hand—that's what they said."

Barney flushed a dark red and suddenly made a great show of looking through his backpack for a book. Kate grinned. She'd long suspected him of having a crush on Melanie—looked as if she was right. And then she stiffened. In her mind she saw Mike dumping worms into tubs. With his left hand.

Two nights later Kate sat at the counter, notepad in front of her, immersed in a new story. One of a collection of stories, this was to be. Mr. Evans probably wouldn't approve—they were definitely not based on anything resembling her own life—but she couldn't care less. He was never going to see them. When the door opened, she didn't pay any attention. Angie was there; she could handle it.

"Hi."

She looked up and her heart made a dive for somewhere around her kneecaps. Mike was standing right over her.

"Hi," she managed. She looked for her mother, but Angie was busy sweeping. She looked tired and was probably in a hurry to get finished and back to her TV.

"What are you doing?" Mike's voice was friendly, his eyes had lost their coldness. He seemed relaxed, looked better. As if he'd been eating and sleeping more lately. He twisted his head around to see her notebook.

"Tales by a Thirteenth Child," he read. *"By Kate Halston.* You? A thirteenth child?"

Kate snatched the book away. "Yes," she answered shortly. "Sort of."

"You are no such thing!" Angie's indignant voice broke in. "You're an only child and you know it. Whatever's gotten into you, Kate?"

Kate felt as if she were on fire from the inside. "I said sort of, Mom," she muttered. "You know. . . . Grandma was a thirteenth child . . . ."

"So what's that got to do with you, I'd like to know?"

"Grandma used to tell stories all the time,

remember? And remember, she said it was because she was a thirteenth child?"

She turned to Mike. "Thirteenth children are gifted that way, she said. Or cursed. Depending on which way you look at it, she said. It's just something they have to do. I was really close to her and I'm like that, I feel just that way. I even look like her—everybody says so . . . ." The rush of words died and her voice petered out.

What in the world am I saying, she thought. And to this guy, of all people. He's going to kill himself laughing at me. To her surprise his face stayed serious.

"Like . . . like her spirit's in you, you mean?"

Kate stared at him, mute with astonishment.

Angie leaned her broom on the counter and sagged down onto one of the stools with a sigh.

"Hogwash," she said. "Just hogwash and you know it, Kate Halston. Good excuse to get out of work."

Kate bridled. With the amount of TV Angie watched, and one excuse after another, Kate worked far more than she did.

"My feet are killing me," Angie moaned. "I'm going into the back. Close up, Kate." She pushed open the swing door. "Thirteenth child, my Aunt Fanny's foot," she grumbled. "What next?"

"Can I read it?" Mike asked, reaching for the notebook.

"No way!" Kate stuffed it out of sight onto a shelf under the counter.

"Don't see the point of writing stories you won't let anybody read," Mike replied. "Never mind," he went on quickly, seeing the look on Kate's face. "I just came by to ask if you wanted more worms. Do you?"

"Yes. We sold out today."

"Okay, I'll drop them by tomorrow morning. I'll have to leave them off early, though. Jed needs me to run one of the boats over to the hotel before breakfast. I'll just leave them in the tubs out back."

"All right," Kate answered.

"They're like to dry out if they don't get into the refrigerator right away," he went on. "Will you water them before you put them in?"

"Sure," Kate said, but she was keeping her voice steady with an effort. When he had reached for her notebook, he had reached with his left hand. For a moment she had forgotten about the robbery; that brought it back like a blow.

The worms were waiting for her when she went out the next morning. The peat moss was dry, so she lined the tubs up in a row, hooked up the hose, and turned the spray on. Absent-mindedly, she started to water them.

Stephanie tensed. This was her first trial and she had to win it. Fame and fortune were hers if she did, but even more important—life! Let this maniac loose onto the streets again and she knew she would be his next victim. His eyes blazed with a hatred so intense they seemed to etch a path of fire across the courtroom, all the way to her. She flinched, but then straightened and stiffened her shoulders. She swept back her riotous mane of blond curls with one hand and turned away from him, toward the jury, with one contemptuous movement.

"Ladies and gentlemen of the jury," she began, her voice ringing with assurance in the echoing courtroom. "You will notice that the defendant swore his oath on the Bible with his left hand? The defendant, ladies and gentlemen, is left-handed! This, as I will prove to you, is essential evidence against him!"

It wasn't until she went to put the tops on the tubs that Kate realized she had drowned the worms.

four

Confessing to Mike the next day was embarrassing.

"You don't have to pay me," he told her.

"Of course I have to pay you. You brought the worms. It was me that drowned them."

"But you'll have to pay me out of your own money. Your dad, he won't pay for dead worms."

Kate's temper flared again. Enough about her dad.

"I goofed. Okay? It's my problem. Can you go back out tonight?"

"Sure."

The gasoline delivery truck pulled in with a massive rumble. Thank goodness her father was out there this afternoon and he could handle it.

Kate heard the driver call out a greeting, and Steve answer.

"By the way . . . ."

Preoccupied with watching what was going on outside, Kate didn't hear Mike at first. The odor of gasoline began to permeate the snack bar. The air conditioner didn't do much about cooling the place, but it sure brought the smells in.

"Kate?"

She turned back to him. "What?"

"I was just thinking. This Saturday I have to take a boat over to those tourist cabins on the lake. Want to come with me?"

A date? This guy was asking her for a date?

As if reading her mind, he went on quickly. "Not a date or anything like that. Just for fun. It's cooler on the lake. Be nice out there. Besides, you'd really be doing me a favor. If you come we can take two boats over, then ride back in one. If I go alone I'll have to hitchhike back."

Kate stared at him, her mind in a turmoil. She wasn't going to go anywhere with him. She wasn't that crazy. And yet. As she hesitated, he tossed his hair back out of his eyes and grinned that grin again. He didn't look dangerous. He looked just like any other guy. In fact, grinning like that, he even looked sort of cute . . . .

Nevertheless. She brought her thoughts up short.

"I have to work here."

"Can't you get someone to take over for you just for once?"

"Dad wouldn't let me."

"Come on. Try. We could swim—maybe take a picnic?"

The thought of the lake was tempting. She lived practically right beside it and hardly ever had a chance to swim in it. She swatted at a fly and pushed her sweaty hair back off her face. She could imagine how cool the water would be. And out on a boat, with a breeze blowing. . . . It was tempting.

"Well?"

"I don't know. I'd have to find someone to come in for me . . . ."

"Great! Meet me down at Jed's at around eight, okay?"

"I didn't say for sure—" But it was too late. Mike had already slammed out.

The driver of the gasoline truck came in and walked up to the counter.

"Burger and fries, okay? And a coffee, large."

"To go or for here?" Kate asked automatically, still staring after Mike.

"I've got time. I'll take it here."

She unwrapped a meat patty and slapped it on the griddle, pulled out a bun, split it, and laid it beside the hamburger, then dumped a basketful of fries into the hot oil. As she stood with the spatula ready to flip the patty, her mind raced. If she could find someone to take her place. . . . If she could catch her dad at a good moment. . . . That would be a miracle. She could wear her bathing suit under her shorts. At that thought she grimaced. Her suit was old and really tacky, faded to a sick green, and so stretched it bagged around the bottom. Nothing she could do about that.

This is not a good idea, a small voice said inside her head. She didn't want to hear it.

The next day at school she looked around and took stock. Who could she ask to take over for her? There were a few girls from her bus she said hello and goodbye to, but she didn't know them well enough to ask them. Just then she was jostled in the crowded hallway, and an elbow prodded her in the ribs.

"What planet are you on now?" a voice asked.

Barney. He hadn't made the bus that morning and she hadn't even thought of him, but he'd do it, she was sure. All he'd been talking about lately was buying that motorcycle. If he was serious about it, he'd be glad of the extra money.

"Barney—you working at the supermarket on Saturday?"

"No . . . ."

"Great. You want to fill in for me at the snack bar?"

Barney hesitated, then seemed to make up his mind. "Sure," he said. The word came out with what seemed like unnecessary force.

Kate looked at him, puzzled for a moment, then shrugged. Whatever was bugging him was his problem. Probably no big deal. Just so long as he could take over for her and let her get away.

"Can you come early? Before eight?"

"Okay."

It was done. And so easy, after all. Now to convince her dad.

When she got off the bus that afternoon Steve was on the pumps. He was gassing up a car and joking with the driver. A good sign. Kate approached him warily as the car pulled out.

"Dad?"

"Yeah?"

"Would it be okay if I took Saturday off? I've got a friend who'll work for me. He's really reliable." She held her breath.

Steve cocked his head, considering. "Sure he'd be okay?"

"Yes, Dad. He's really a good guy."

"Boyfriend, eh? Didn't know you had one."

"No, Dad. Nothing like that. He's just a friend."

Her father winked. "Sure. I'll bet."

"Dad, if he was a boyfriend I'd be going out with him, wouldn't I? He wouldn't be taking over for me."

"Where are you going, anyway?"

Darn. She didn't want to get into that.

"Swimming. It's so hot. Would it be all right, Dad? Please?" Kate held her breath, surprised herself at how important this was to her.

"I guess so. Fact is, I wouldn't mind taking a break myself. He can do the pumps too. Might as well work for his money, this 'not-a-boyfriend' of yours."

Relief flooded through her, followed by a quick pang of guilt. Barney sure would work for his money if he had to tend the snack bar and pump gas. She knew that from past experience. And on Saturdays Angie usually disappeared off to the mall; she wouldn't be much help.

She felt guilty all over again on Saturday morning, but the excitement overrode it. Calm down, Kate, she told herself. It's just a boat ride, for Pete's sake. But she found herself humming as she dug a clean towel out of the laundry and started to throw together a few sandwiches. The air conditioner seemed to have given up entirely, and the temperature inside the snack bar was almost unbearable. Keeping the door open didn't help at all. The heat shimmered outside; the air itself smelled hot—rubbery and thick. That lake was going to feel so good!

She was out of there as soon as Barney arrived and she had shown him what to do. Her father had come in late the night before in a foul mood. The pickup had needed some repairs and that had set him off again, although he didn't need much excuse these days to go on a binge.

We're short of money, so he goes out and throws away what we do have on booze, Kate thought in disgust. He was sleeping in now and she didn't want to be around when he got up. He'd probably change his mind just out of bad temper and make her stay after all. She got her bike out of the garage and pedaled off.

The motorcycle dealership was on the way to Jed's. There weren't any bikers around this early, so she pedaled in to see the bike in the window that Barney had been raving about. Looked pretty ordinary to her. Barney was a straight-A student, read more books than she did, and hated sports. Why in the world would he want that? But then, why would anybody want a motorcycle? If she had the money she'd buy a car. A sports car. A Mercedes, maybe . . . .

A motorcycle roared in and pulled up beside her. It backfired as the rider cut the engine.

The image of a flaming red Mercedes convertible, Kate at the wheel, hair flying in the wind, shattered.

"Want something? Just about to open up." The biker was an older man with long, surprisingly well-kept, shoulder-length hair. He was wearing a muscle shirt and no jacket. Kate could see a purple snake writhing across the biceps of his right arm. He grinned at her.

"No. Just passing by," Kate stammered. She tore her eyes away from the snake with an effort, fumbled for the pedal, hit her instep on it, and rode off. In her hurry she almost overbalanced and the bike gave an alarming wobble. A laugh rang out behind her.

Any traces of leftover guilt dissolved completely as soon as Kate got out on the lake. In fact, she forgot Barney completely. She putted along in her boat, following in the wake of Mike's. The shore fell away behind them, the wind dried the streams of sweat that had made her shirt cling to her body. The snack bar, her father, her mother—they all disappeared as well. Free! For one day, anyway, she was free.

Too soon, as far as she was concerned, they reached their destination. They tied the boats up at the dock where the tourist cabins were, then went searching for the office. The cabins were run-down and shabby, but they seemed to be full up. There were kids all over the place, all of them screaming, people fishing off the dock, and more people splashing in the shallow water off the beach. A lifeguard, tanned deep mahogany, lounged on his lookout with eyes closed. He might have been asleep. As they walked away from the lake, toward the trees, mosquitoes divebombed them mercilessly. Kate began to scratch. She couldn't wait to deliver the boat and get into the water herself.

They found a wooden arrow with "OFF CE" stenciled on it, the "I" so faded it was illegible, and followed along the direction it pointed, through a row of cottages strewn with bathing suits and towels hanging on veranda railings and lines strung between the trees. The cottages all had names: Moonglow, Snooz'In, Lazy Daze, Livin' Ezy, C'mon Inn. The last one was more pretentious: Holiday Inn. Not quite, Kate thought with a grin. A sign on its door proclaimed it to be the office, however, missing "i" and all.

Kate settled herself on a stump outside the door while Mike went in to settle up about the boat. The air here was fresh and redolent with the scent of pine trees. It was shady where she sat, and a breeze off the lake made the heat not only bearable, but almost comfortable. A young tabby cat poured itself out of a window beside her and rubbed up against her legs. She stroked it absent-mindedly. Its fur felt soft and sensuous against her bare skin. That's what a mink coat must feel like, Kate thought.

Stephanie felt the rich fur against her bare arms. She couldn't resist sinking her face into it, rubbing her cheek against it. Never had she ever imagined anything could feel so soft! Then she straightened and, majestically, threw the coat back at the tall figure in the doorway.

"It would take more than this to bribe me!" she proclaimed haughtily. "Take your filthy mink and be gone. Besides—killing animals for their fur is inhumane, you beast!"

"Another Thirteenth Child tale in the making?"

Kate shot up from the stump; the cat streaked out of sight into the trees.

"I was just resting—"

"You had that look on your face. That 'million miles away' look."

What made him think he knew her that well? But Kate was in too good a mood to get mad.

"You want to take a swim now?"

"I sure do," she answered. "But not here, it's too crowded. Let's take the boat farther down the lake. I know where there's a good beach. There'll probably be some people there—always are—but not nearly as many as here."

They were in luck. There was only one family, picnicking down at the end of the beach. Mike and Kate tied up the boat and spread their towels on the sand. Kate pulled off her sweat-soaked shirt and her shorts and plunged into the lake. She gasped at the shock of the still-cold water, then struck out swimming. Mike stripped down to his cutoffs and dove in after her. When she was used to it and had got her breath back, Kate relaxed and let herself float, eyes closed, face up into the sun. The water felt cool and silken around her—she abandoned herself to it luxuriously. Mike surfaced beside her, treading water.

"What was it about?" he asked.

"What was what about?" Kate answered lazily.

"Your story. The one you were making up back there."

Kate opened her eyes, let her feet sink down, and began to tread water as well. "Nothing."

"You spend all your time making up stories?"

"No. Of course not."

"What about friends? I never see any other kids hanging around."

"I don't know many kids at school yet."

"No boyfriends?"

What was it with people and boyfriends, anyway?

"No," she answered shortly. "I've got better things to do with my time." The wake from a water-skiing boat farther out hit her and she swallowed a mouthful of water. She coughed and shook her head angrily.

She'd be sixteen in a couple of months. Sweet sixteen and never been kissed. Sounded like something out of the fifties.

"An escape. Isn't that what they call it? When you can't face real life and spend all your time making up things?"

Kate glared at him. "It's not like that at all. Nothing like that." Another wave caught her in the face and she choked down water. Her eyes were suddenly stinging. She ducked her head back in the water, shook her hair out of her face, then struck out for shore.

What gave him the right to criticize her anyway? Not everybody was obsessed with sex.

She'd never had a real date. None of the guys at school seemed to know she was alive. Not that she cared. She had her own things to do. And her stories weren't an escape. Even if they were—so what? What was so great about real life?

By the time he followed her onto the beach she had dried herself off and brought out the sandwiches. Her face was carefully blank. She was feeling rather proud of her self-composure, in fact. If her heart was beating in heavy thumping lurches, and there was a tight pain all around it, he'd never know.

Mike threw himself down beside her.

"You're not mad, are you? About what I said?"

"Of course not. Why should I be?"

"It's just. . . you're so pretty. I would've thought there'd be guys hanging around all the time."

Yeah, sure, Kate thought. Five minutes with my dad and they'd be history. Then she realized what he'd said. Pretty? She felt the blood rush to her face. She grabbed up her towel, tossed her hair forward, and began to rub it vigorously. It was just a line, of course. He didn't mean it— naturally, he didn't. Pretty was the last thing she saw when she looked in the mirror. Still. . . .

"What about you?" she stammered finally.

"What about me?" he answered.

"Well—where do you come from? Why did you leave? That sort of thing." Do *you* have a girlfriend, her mind added silently.

Mike rolled onto his back and closed his eyes. For a moment she thought he wasn't going to answer.

"Come from a small town near Ottawa you've probably never even heard of," he said finally. "My mom and I didn't get along, school and I didn't get along, and I'm old enough to quit if I want to, so I just left. That's it. Pretty boring, eh?"

"That's not escaping?" She couldn't resist.

"Nope. Unfortunately not. I'm still here."

His voice turned dull. A frown creased

between his eyes, and Kate was suddenly reminded of how he had looked when he had first slammed into the snack bar. She pushed that out of her mind. She didn't want to think about that today.

"Wasn't there anybody?" The question slipped out in spite of herself.

"There was a girl . . . ."

Kate's heart took a lurch. She looked away quickly and concentrated on picking at a fraying edge of the towel.

"A girl?" She really didn't want to hear this, but couldn't stop herself.

"Stacy." His voice was so low she could hardly hear him, almost as if he had forgotten about her and was talking to himself. He rolled over and buried his face in his towel.

Kate dared a look at him. There was sand on his back, rough against the glistening wetness of his skin. She caught herself just before reaching over to brush it off.

"What about her?"

"Something happened . . . ." Mike suddenly seemed to realize what he was saying. He sat up so quickly Kate had to pull herself back. She'd been unconsciously leaning toward him.

"Hey. No big deal," he said. "I brought some sandwiches too. Let's eat."

The frown was gone, the grin back. Put on like a mask, Kate couldn't help thinking.

five

Barney was gassing up a Toyota when Kate got
back. She waved to him, then went on into the
snack bar. A few minutes later he followed her.

"I'm beat," he announced. "Wiped out. Cars
coming in and out all day." Dramatically, he slid
down behind the counter and stretched his long
and lanky body out on the floor, back draped
against the wall. The couple from the Toyota
came in and stared at him curiously.

"The help has a case of terminal tired," Kate
said. "What can I get you?"

After they left, she paid Barney from the till.
"You can quit now if you want," she said. "I'll
take over."

"Thanks, Kate." He counted the money, folded it carefully, put it in his pocket, and gave the pocket a satisfied pat. "Getting there," he said.

Kate turned on the water for the sink and squirted detergent in. When would they ever be able to afford a dishwasher? She was sweating again, and the day on the lake was already just a memory.

"That Honda," Barney went on in a dreamy voice. "Can't you just see me bootin' to school on that?"

"'Bootin' to school'?" Kate fought down a smile. "Barney, how much time have you been spending around those bikers, anyway?"

"That sure would make people stand up and take notice, wouldn't it? People like Melanie Davis?"

Melanie Davis again? He really was stuck on her. Irrationally, Kate felt a stab of annoyance. It was none of her business, but still. . . . It was so typical. Half the guys in the school followed Melanie around like puppy dogs. She thought Barney would have more sense.

"You're aiming high." In spite of herself, there was an edge of sarcasm to her words.

Barney didn't seem to notice it. "You going to dream about something impossible, you might as well dream big," he answered. The words were offhand—joking—but there was something about his face that looked serious.

Guys. Kate turned off the water with a vicious twist. Sheep, more like it. Even Barney.

"My mom shown up yet?" she asked.

"No. I haven't seen her all day."

"Not even this morning? Before she went out?"

"Nope. Far as I know, she didn't ever go out."

That was unusual. "What about my dad?"

"He left early. Hasn't come back yet." Barney's voice was carefully controlled, but his face suddenly closed.

"Did he say anything to you?"

"Asked where you were. When I said you'd already gone he just sort of grunted at me and left. I don't think he was in too good a mood."

That's probably the understatement of the year, Kate thought.

"Stay on just a couple of minutes more, will you, Barn? I'm going to go check and see where Mom is. She might have gone out and then come in the back way and you didn't notice. She's usually around here by now." It wasn't like Angie not to at least put in an appearance at the snack bar on a Saturday.

She found Angie upstairs, lying on her bed. Her face was turned to the wall and she was still in her nightgown. It looked as if she hadn't been up all day.

"Mom?" Kate hesitated at her bedroom door. "Are you all right?"

"I'm not feeling too good. Just a little tired, I guess." She didn't turn to look at Kate.

"Mom!" This was definitely not usual. "Should I call a doctor?"

"No!" The response was sharp. "I'll be all right, Kate. I just need to rest up. I'll be better tomorrow—just leave me alone now, okay?" She waved a hand over her shoulder at Kate.

"Leave me *alone*, Kate," she repeated, when Kate made no move to go.

Reluctantly, Kate closed the door and went back downstairs. For all her complaining, Angie was hardly ever sick, and when she was, she was usually off to a doctor at the first symptom.

"My mom's upstairs," Kate said to Barney as she pushed through the door into the snack bar.

He looked at her. There must have been something showing in her face.

"Is anything wrong?" he asked.

"No," she answered, too quickly. "It's all right."

"If I can do anything . . . ?"

"No," she repeated. "It's fine. Really." Suddenly all she wanted was for him to leave, but as he turned to go, the door opened and his father pushed in.

"So! This is where you've been all day!"

Kate was startled by the anger in his voice. She knew Barney's parents only slightly. His father was the kind of man who always seemed to be in too much of a hurry to speak to anyone. He had a consulting business that he ran out of his home, and seemed to spend a lot of his time in Toronto. He wasn't really friendly with anyone in town. Barney's mother was even more of a mystery. She dressed like someone out of

Vogue magazine, and spent most of her time someplace else as well. She didn't even shop in town—rumor had it she ordered most of their stuff by phone from the city.

They must be pretty rich, Kate thought. It hadn't occurred to her before. Mr. Phillips drove a Thunderbird and Mrs. Phillips had a sports car. How come Barney couldn't afford his motorcycle, then?

"You were supposed to spend the day studying, young man," Mr. Phillips thundered. "It's Saturday, remember? Why else did you quit working at that ridiculous supermarket job?"

"Quit?" Barney's voice was bitter. "I didn't exactly quit, did I? *You* called up the manager and told him I wouldn't be coming in anymore."

"That's enough! Your marks drop—you work harder. It's as simple as that. I told you I want you in your room studying every Saturday and Sunday until you pull them back up."

"Dad—" Barney sounded desperate. "From a 95% to a 90% in English, that's not such a big deal!"

"It is to me, young man. You want to get into a top university, you have to get top marks." Mr. Phillips turned to glare at Kate. "Running around with local girls isn't going to get you anywhere except into trouble."

Kate felt heat blaze in her cheeks. "He was just working for the day—" she began.

"Which I expressly forbade." He dismissed her with a contemptuous glance. "This is none of your business, anyway."

"I beg your pardon!" Kate exploded, then she saw Barney's face. He looked as if he wished he could die right on the spot. A wave of sympathy washed over her. She bit back the words she'd been about to hurl at his father.

"Thanks, Barney," she said instead. "You really helped me out today." She glared back at Mr. Phillips, then turned on her heel and slammed into their own kitchen.

As the door closed behind her, she grabbed her elbows and hugged her arms tightly to her. She was shaking with rage. How dare that man! Poor Barney—if that was what he had to put up with at home.

Her father came in even later than he had the evening before. Kate heard the pickup crunch over the gravel at the side of the station, then skid to a stop right below her window with a squeal of brakes. He came heavily up the stairs. She heard him stumble, then a loud curse. He went into the room he shared with her mother. An argument began—louder and angrier than usual. Suddenly Angie cried out. Kate could stand it no longer—she was sure she had heard a slap. Without thinking, she jumped up, ran out, and banged on the door of her parents' room.

"Dad! Mom! What's going on in there?"

Their door was wrenched open and her father stood framed in the light from a single bedlamp. Kate quailed. He looked furious—out of control.

"Get out of here!" he shouted, the words slurring together. "This is none of your business!"

"Dad! What are you doing?" Kate looked past him, horrified, to her mother. Angie was lying on the floor, curled up into a ball. As Kate watched, however, she put one hand on the bed for support and pulled herself up onto it.

"I fell, Kate. I tripped and fell. Now do as your dad says. Get out of here. He's upset— you're only making things worse."

"Mom! I can't leave you . . . ."

"You heard her, get out!" Steve roared. "Get back to your own room and don't meddle in things that don't concern you."

"My mother concerns me," Kate began hotly, then cringed back in spite of herself as her father lifted one raised fist. He took the opportunity to slam the door. Kate heard the lock click.

"Mom!" She pounded on the door.

"It's all right now, Kate. Just go away and everything will be all right." Angie's voice was desperate.

Kate sank down to the floor outside the door. She pressed her ear to the peeling, paint-covered wood.

"You never let me forget, do you?" she heard Steve rant.

"No, Steve, I didn't mean . . . ."

"Whining all the time. . . . Blaming me. . . ."

"I never blamed you, Steve. I didn't! You know that."

"You blame me every time you look at me. Think I don't know? Think I can't tell?"

"You're imagining—"

Kate's mouth was dry. She tried to swallow, but couldn't. Her heart seemed to be trying to tear itself out of her chest. The same old argument. The same old words. Would it never end?

"Go ahead. You're right. I am a failure. I ruined everything for all of us. Go ahead, say it. Everybody else does. *Say it!*"

Angie answered, something too low for Kate to hear. It sounded placating. Comforting. *She* was comforting *him*?

Gradually, both voices ceased. Gradually, the room behind the door became silent. Kate huddled outside it. She didn't seem to be able to move. When the first rays of dawn began to streak through the hall window, she was still there, cramped with pain.

Mike turned up the next morning carrying a billboard. Kate was tending the snack bar. Her father had stormed through the kitchen earlier on, then headed for the room above the garage. Kate hadn't spoken to him, didn't even care what he was doing there. She knocked on her parents' bedroom door as soon as he was safely out of the way, but Angie just called that she would be out later. Kate didn't know what to do. At least her mom sounded all right.

"I got an idea, Kate. What do you think of this?"

Kate looked up without interest. The big, square billboard stood propped up by a backpiece. It was white, and painted on it in black were two smiling worms. They were standing happily up on their tails, mortarboards with dangling tassels perched rakishly on their heads.

EDUCATED WORMS!

the sign proclaimed in huge letters.

GUARANTEED GRADUATES
OF THE MOST ADVANCED—
THE *ONLY*—WRIGGLE SCHOOL AROUND!

"Thought we should add some class to the business," Mike said. Kate didn't answer.

"Hey, what's the matter?"

"Nothing," she muttered. Her head was pounding and she felt sick.

"You sure?" He took a closer look at her. "You look terrible."

So much for pretty. "I didn't sleep too well."

A car pulled in front of the pumps and honked impatiently. Kate grabbed up a dishtowel to dry her hands and started out.

"Where's your dad? Isn't he here today?"

"He's. . . . He's busy." Her eyes strayed to the garage. Mike's followed. He frowned.

"Got the day off today, I'll do the pumps for you," he said.

"There's no need," Kate began, but at that moment two men came in.

"Anybody pumping gas?" one asked.

"Any coffee around?" the other one put in.

Kate looked at Mike, then gave a shrug of resignation and nodded. "Okay, go ahead. Thanks."

"Be right with you," Mike said. He shouldered his sign and headed for the door. The first man followed him out.

"Need any worms?" Kate heard Mike ask. "We got the best around." He placed the sign where people driving by could see it. The man looked at it and shouted with laughter.

"Hey, Mack!" he called back. "Get a couple tubs of them worms, will you? Let's see we can't outsmart the fish today!" He went on out to his battered, ancient Plymouth, still chortling. Mike made a thumbs-up sign behind his back to Kate.

Sunday was usually a busy day. The regulars weren't likely to come in, but there were always a bunch of tourists. Today was no exception. By noon, Kate was exhausted. The room was full, and the air thick with smoke, when she heard the roar of motorcycles. They peeled off the road and skidded to a stop outside the snack bar. The door opened; four bikers strode in. One of the small tables crowded into the space between the counter and the door was free, and they slumped down into the chairs around it. Kate saw the man she'd seen at the motorcycle dealership. With luck, he wouldn't recognize her.

Reluctantly, she went over to the table to get their order.

"What happened to J.D.?" The speaker was the youngest of the group. He was the only one wearing a jacket. A large black and white spider was painted crudely on the back of it, legs extended to crawl over his shoulders and around his waist. He was sweating profusely.

Probably thinks he's too cool to take it off, Kate thought. For some reason, she took an immediate dislike to him. There was a mean look to his eyes.

"Dropped his bike the other day." That was the man she'd seen outside the store. He looked up at her. "Hey—I know you, don't I? You were around the place the other day. Want to buy a bike?" The words were teasing, but in a friendly way.

Kate clutched her order pad. "No," she answered. "I was just looking. What'll you guys have?"

"BEER!" the other three chorused.

"We don't have . . . ."

"Lay off, you guys. Cokes all round will be fine. Name's Ed. What's yours?"

"Kate. Anything else?" She looked out the window but couldn't see Mike. Where was he, anyway?

"Sure, I'll have a burger."

"Fries."

"Chips. You got a package of barbecue chips?" Kate scribbled furiously.

"Burger for me too, doll-baby," the younger one

drawled. His eyes traveled from Kate's face down to her feet and back up again, then he turned to the older man as if bored by what he'd seen.

Kate clenched her teeth until it hurt.

"That was a pretty good ride, Bud. Go for another boot tomorrow?"

"Naw. Gotta work."

"You working? What you doing that for?"

A chorus of laughter. Kate took advantage of it to escape back to the bar, acutely conscious that the young biker's eyes were back on her. The others might be normal—or "almost"—but there was definitely something weird about him.

Angie appeared just as the bikers were leaving. She made herself a cup of coffee and headed back up to her room before Kate had a chance to say anything to her. Steve didn't appear at all.

Around evening, the snack bar emptied. Kate opened the door to try to get rid of the combined, almost overwhelming miasma of grease and smoke. The air conditioner was completely useless as far as that was concerned. Mike ambled in and sat on a stool by the counter. Kate sighed and sank down onto the stool behind, fanning herself half-heartedly with a menu. Tired as she was, she couldn't get out of her mind the picture that had been tormenting her all day. The picture of her mother on the floor, her father standing over her almost crazy with anger. She knew her father's temper. She and Angie both knew it. Feared it, and with good reason.

Absent-mindedly, she poured two cups of coffee and slid one over to Mike. She should offer to pay him. Before she could say anything, however, the door opened and her father staggered in. He was stubble-cheeked and reeked of beer. Kate's face flamed with embarrassment.

"Hi, Mr. Halston—" Mike began, but Steve just pushed on past into the kitchen.

"Angie!" they heard him bellow. "Where the hell are you?"

"Your dad really got wasted last night, by the looks of it, eh?" Mike shook his head, grinning.

Kate froze. "You really can't keep your mouth shut about things that aren't any of your business, can you?" she demanded.

Mike stared at her, surprised. "Doesn't matter a squirrel's hind leg to me what your dad does," he said. "Anyways, who doesn't get drunk on a Saturday night? Most people I know do."

"Angie! Get the hell down here! I mean now!"

Mike looked more closely at Kate.

"Your mom all right?" he asked. "I mean—he didn't knock her around or anything, did he?"

"Get out of here." The words were ice-cold. So brittle they seemed to cut the air. "Maybe thieves who hold up snack bars and drugstores hang out with drunks who beat up on their wives, but it's not like that around here. Get out and don't come back."

Mike leaped to his feet. His eyes turned as cold as Kate's voice. Suddenly, he looked dangerous. Kate felt a stab of fear. He jammed his hand into his pocket. Kate stopped breathing.

"For the coffee," he said, throwing a handful of change onto the counter. "I wouldn't want to owe you." He turned on his heel and slammed out.

six

Kate had a dream that night. She dreamed that she woke up and her room was pitch dark—she couldn't even see the outline of the window. In her dream, she sat up, every part of her prickling and crawling with some unnameable dread. She reached out for her bedside lamp. There was emptiness where it should have been. The darkness all around her was absolute. Slowly, she lowered her feet over the side of the bed. She didn't want to leave the safety of it, but she had to. She had to find the door—had to get out. Arms outstretched, she began to feel along the wall to where she knew it should be. Nothing. Confused, dread rapidly escalating to panic, she reached a corner and felt along that wall. No door. No bookcase, either. Or desk. Or chair. It wasn't until she had traversed all four walls, and then started over again, that her mind accepted the horrifying reality. There wasn't a door anymore. There wasn't a window. Even the bed had now disappeared. There was nothing. She was closed in, trapped in the empty blackness with no way out. She screamed . . . .

And woke up. Covered in sweat, weak and shaking.

She slept no more that night. When the alarm went off, she slapped it quiet and turned away. She didn't want to get up. If her mother could do it, why couldn't she? She didn't want to face either of her parents. She didn't want to face anything.

Exam review week, she suddenly remembered. She couldn't miss school. Exams were coming up—she'd done well all year, she couldn't let up now. Reluctantly, feeling as weighed down with fatigue as an old woman, she clambered out of bed.

To her surprise, when she went down to the kitchen her father was already there, pouring himself a cup of coffee. He had shaved, his hair was neatly combed back, and he was wearing clean jeans and T-shirt. Warily, not meeting his eyes, Kate took down the cereal from the cupboard and went to the refrigerator for milk. She poured a glass of orange juice and sat down at the table. Steve brought his coffee over and set it down on the table opposite her. His hands were shaking so badly he spilled almost half of it into the saucer. He sat down heavily.

"I got to apologize, Kate," he said in a low voice, mopping at the coffee with a paper towel. "I was out of line Saturday night. Way out of line." He paused, still looking down at his coffee. Kate didn't answer.

"It's not going to happen again, Kate—I promise."

Finally, Kate raised her eyes. He looked up and met them.

"I promise, Kate," he repeated. "No more booze. It's the booze that does it. I'm going off it. Things are going to be different—you'll see. I know it can't ever be the way it used to be—the money's all gone—but it's going to be different. Better. It's going to be better." His eyes were pleading.

He looks pathetic, Kate thought. Suddenly she felt as if she were the parent and he the child. Then she closed herself off. She'd heard those promises before. He never kept them. Never could keep off the booze for longer than a day—couple of days at the most. It was too painful, hoping *this* was the time he meant it— she'd believe it when she saw it, not before.

Angie came in. She too had made an effort to fix herself up. Crimson lipstick looked garish against the pallor of her face, but she had tied her hair back with a ribbon and was wearing a light, flowered housecoat.

"Morning, Kate," Angie said. Her voice was shrill and unnaturally bright. "Mind you eat a good breakfast now, and don't forget your lunch today. Got to keep up your strength for your exams. If you want to get into a good university, your high school record is pretty important."

Kate looked at her incredulously. Even now Angie could just pretend nothing had happened. And since when had she ever cared about Kate getting into a good university, let alone any university at all? Any time Kate had mentioned it, all Angie had done was complain about how much it would cost. Her father, of course, wouldn't even talk about it. He sure wasn't like Barney's dad. Get a scholarship, though, they wouldn't be able to stop her.

Just the thought of it. In her mind she could see herself walking down a shady, tree-lined path, backpack filled with books, other students hurrying around her. A totally new life . . . .

If she ever got away from here, she'd never come back.

When Kate got off the bus that afternoon and headed toward the service station she was still wary. What would she find? Her father, however, was out tending the pumps, talking and joking with Bob Dowles and Norris Lamont. Angie was behind the counter, looking as if she didn't have a worry in the world. It was Burrell's delivery day again, and she was even flirting a bit with

Rob. The relief was enormous. Perhaps things would turn around after all. It was possible. Her parents had used to be so happy together . . . .

Yeah. And pigs can fly. Take advantage of the cease-fire, she told herself cynically. It probably won't last long.

They were out of worms. That made her face something she'd been avoiding all day: Mike. No matter how much she tried to put the blame on him, she had to admit she'd had no right to explode at him that way. She owed him for a day's work, and she owed him an apology. She squirmed at the thought of it, but there was no way out.

"Mom," she said. "I've got to go into town. Can you stay on for a while? I'll take over soon as I get back, okay?"

"Sure, honey," Angie answered.

"Hi, Kate," Rob put in. "You're looking good today."

The guy was getting old. He must be blind as well. If she looked half as bad as she felt, something a cat wouldn't bother to drag in would look better. She dug up a smile, anyway.

"Thanks, Rob. Had your glasses checked lately?"

She grabbed her bike out of the garage and set off for Jed's place. As she pedaled along the shoulder of the highway, she began to rehearse what she was going to say to Mike. Nothing came out right. The closer she got, the more panicky she got. This was not going to be easy. A car swept past her, sending small pebbles flying and causing her to lose control for a moment. It had nearly sideswiped her. What if it had . . . ?

Kate lay in the hospital, swathed in bandages from head to toe. Only her face peered out, unscathed, but white and drawn with pain.

"You can only stay a minute," the quiet voice of a nurse said in the doorway. "She's not out of danger yet."

Mike tiptoed in. "Kate," he whispered. "I'm so sorry about the accident. So sorry you were hurt."

"I was coming . . ." Kate gasped back weakly, "coming to apologize to you . . . ."

"Apologize! Kate, there's nothing to apologize for! Just live, Kate. LIVE!"

Unfortunately Jed's place loomed up ahead of her and Kate was still in one piece. Even more unfortunately, Mike was standing right there, watching her pedal in. She pulled up beside him.

"Mike," she began.

He stared back at her silently. His eyes were still cold, but controlled now. He'd lost the dangerous look that had frightened her so. But how far away was it?

"Look," she forced out. "About what I said . . . I . . . I'm sorry . . . ."

"Why? Need more worms?"

Kate flushed and anger surged up again. She swallowed hard and fought it down.

"Well, we do, but that's not it. I mean. . . I shouldn't have said what I did. About thieves and that . . . ." Her voice died out.

"Why not? It's what you think. I'm not your sort of people. Far as you're concerned I'm just a thief, and not even a good one at that."

"No. Mike—"

"I'll bring you some worms tomorrow, don't worry."

"But, Mike—I'm really sorry . . . ."

"Glad to hear it. Great. Okay." He turned away. "Look, I've got work to do," he threw back over his shoulder. "See you tomorrow." He strode off down the path to the lake.

Kate watched him go. He hadn't even given her time to offer him the day's pay.

Fine. If that's the way he wants it, that's okay by me, she thought. I couldn't care less. He comes from scummy people, he behaves like scum. Who cares?

But pedaling back to the garage seemed to take forever and every bit of energy she had. The sun beat down mercilessly; there wasn't even a hint of a breeze. Halfway there her shirt was already soaked with sweat and clinging to her back. A couple of wolf-whistles as she passed by the gang around the motorcycle dealership didn't help. When she finally let herself in through the back door to the kitchen, her head was aching again and she was in a foul mood.

Her father was sitting at the table with a bottle of beer in his hand. He started up guiltily when she came in.

"Not what you think, Kate," he said hurriedly.

"I meant what I said this morning. It's just. . . it's so hot." He gave her a shamefaced grin and an apologetic shrug. "And to tell the truth, Kate, I've still got sort of a hangover. No matter what your mother says, a hair of the dog doesn't hurt. Just one little beer. That doesn't mean anything . . . ."

Kate slammed out of the kitchen into the snack bar. She threw herself down on the stool behind the counter and buried her face in her arms.

"You were gone a long time. I've missed all of 'General Hospital' and most of 'Oprah.'"

Rob had left and Angie was tidying up one of the tables. Her good mood seemed to have dissolved. Her face was pinched and the whine was back in her voice. The cartons of groceries were still stacked by the door.

"Finish unpacking for me, will you?" She glanced nervously at the kitchen door. The ribbon she'd pulled her hair back with had come half-untied and was hanging limply down her back, letting her hair escape in untidy strands. So much for things being different from now on.

To get out of here. To get out of here. *To get out of here!* A whole new life. A whole different life. Kate's head swam. Her mind blocked out her mother, the snack bar, her father in the kitchen with his beer. Everything. She wasn't here anymore. She could see herself—older, successful, beautifully dressed. Courted by rich, famous men.

"Why do you never mention your home, Kathryn?" they would ask. (She would have

changed her name by then.) *"Your family?"*

"I have no home," she would answer. *"I have no family."*

When she finally stumbled up to bed that night, her schoolbooks still lay where she had tossed them when she had come in. There were two review tests the next day. She hadn't studied for either of them.

I don't care, she thought as she turned off the light and pulled the covers up between herself and the world. I just don't care.

The rest of the week passed in a daze. She couldn't concentrate. Exams came; she wrote them. It was as if she weren't really there at all, but somewhere outside herself, just watching. It was almost a shock to find out she had done well in spite of everything.

Summer holidays meant spending all day every day in the snack bar instead of just Saturdays and Sundays and after school. Mike turned up with worms about twice a week. She paid him, he thanked her, and they were both very polite to each other, but they didn't talk much. Once or twice Kate caught him looking at her with a strange expression, but when she did he looked away quickly and made any kind of an excuse to get away from her.

Her father was drinking again. Trying to hide it, but spending more and more time in the room over the garage. When he did, Kate had to tend the pumps and Angie took over in the snack bar sullenly. She'd obviously given up the brief hope she'd had, and seemed depressed, spending more and more time in front of the TV.

"Can you take over for a while, Kate?" she asked one day when there was a lull at the pumps. "I've really had it today."

For the first time since school had let out, Kate took a good look at her. Angie didn't look well. Her skin was pasty and her eyes looked dark and sunken. Her hair hung in limp strands. She wiped at her forehead with the back of her arm, and slumped on the counter. Kate was moved in spite of herself. Her mom was—what? Not even forty yet. She looked so much older. She looked so hopeless.

"Take off, Mom," Kate said. "I can manage."

"Thanks, Kate." Angie headed toward the kitchen with a sigh of relief.

"Mom?"

"Yes?" She turned, with one hand already on the swinging door, her face blank.

What was it Kate wanted to say?

I'm sorry.

That was crazy. Sorry for what?

Sorry for everything.

She didn't say it. Angie looked questioningly at her for a moment. Kate shrugged.

"Nothing. Forget it."

Angie went on into the other room. Seconds later the TV blared out.

Kate looked down at her hands. Her nails were chipped and broken. There was a hangnail on her thumb. She pulled at it with her teeth. The piece of flesh ripped off and there was sudden pain, a pain too great and out of all proportion to such a small wound.

The heat wave didn't let up in spite of a couple of thundershowers that just turned everything into a steam bath. Half the time Kate felt she was dragging herself through air as viscous and heavy as soup. On the first of July there was to be a parade and fireworks on the town beach at night. She had no intention of going, but Barney turned up after lunch with other ideas.

"Come on, Kate," he said. "Get your mom to take over and grab your bathing suit. We can swim, stuff ourselves silly with hot dogs, and watch the fireworks. Everybody will be there."

"I don't want to, Barn," she said. "I'm going to bed early."

"Kate, I haven't seen you since school let out. You can't just spend all your time here. Come on—it'll be fun!"

The more she argued, the more he insisted. When he even went so far as to get Angie to agree, albeit reluctantly, to take over, she finally gave up.

"You win, Barn," she sighed. "You really know how to get what you want, don't you?" For a moment she wondered why he *did* want her to go with him so much, then pushed the thought out of her mind. Understanding Barney was just too much work.

"Get what I want?" he echoed. "I wish!" The tone of his voice was joking, lighthearted, but for a moment his eyes went as hard and blank as Mike's. Kate was suddenly disconcerted.

When they reached the town, however, Barney's enthusiasm returned to the point where it was almost feverish. It was contagious, and, despite her conviction that she wasn't going to enjoy herself, when the parade started she found her feet keeping time to the music in spite of herself.

"Now aren't you glad you came?" Barney asked later on, as they sat side by side on the beach after their swim. The lake was still chilly enough to make the sun actually feel good.

"I guess," Kate admitted. "Thanks, Barn, for dragging me out. You're a good guy."

"You bet," Barney agreed. "The greatest. Now, if you could just convince Melanie Davis of that, you'd be doing me a real favor." He looked over at a group of kids sitting on blankets near them.

The group had parked their car as close to the beach as possible, taken the stereo speakers, and propped them up on the roof. Music blasted out at an unbelievable level. Any other day the police would have turfed them out in seconds, but this day they could get away with it, it seemed. Melanie Davis was one of them, and Barney's eyes were fixed on her. Melanie, fully aware that most of the boys around her, as well as Barney, were looking at her, lay back with an exaggerated sigh. She flipped her hair away from her face, loosened the straps of her bikini top, and slipped them over her shoulders.

So that was it. That was why he'd been so insistent on her coming here with him. He just wanted to see Melanie. And have Melanie see him. With her. Was he hoping to make Melanie jealous? Lots of luck. The corners of Kate's mouth twitched down. She brushed sand off her legs irritably and tugged at her grungy green bathing suit. As if anybody would be jealous of her in *that*, anyway.

Why should I care, she thought. It's not as if I had a crush on him or anything. He's just a friend. But still, deep down inside, no matter how ridiculous she told herself she was being, she felt betrayed.

The fireworks were to begin as soon as it was dark. Kate and Barney found a spot from which to watch them and settled down. As Kate glanced around, waiting for the show to begin, she saw Mike sitting by himself near the dock. He saw her at the same moment. For an instant she was tempted to call to him, even lifted her hand to wave, then Barney grabbed her arm.

"Look," he shouted. "They're starting!"

Kate jumped as the first bomb burst exploded overhead. Her eyes were drawn immediately to the shower of multicolored stars falling toward them, but not before she had seen Mike half rise as if about to come over to her, then sink back down when she didn't wave after all.

Not my problem, she thought, and soon forgot about him.

When the fireworks were over and she and Barney went to retrieve their bikes, she remembered him and looked for him back at the dock. He wasn't there.

The next morning, the Davidson boy was through the door the moment she opened up.

"Another robbery!" he told her, bursting with the importance of being the first to bear the news.

A small variety store had been held up at around midnight. The thief had been wearing a ski mask and had brandished a knife. It was a family-owned business and the owner had made the mistake of trying to fight. The thief had stabbed him in the arm before taking off with everything in the cash register.

"It's one of those bikers, I'll bet." The group of regulars had come to their own conclusions around their table that afternoon.

"No way," Barney countered, when Kate told him what the talk was. "They're good guys. They wouldn't do anything like that. It's somebody from out of town. Has to be."

seven

A couple of days later Kate was surprised to see Jed's pickup pull into the station just as she finished gassing up a car. Mike eased himself out of the cab.

"Hi," he said.

"Hi," Kate answered.

"I . . . ." He shrugged and tossed his hair back out of his eyes. "I brought something. Peace offering, sort of." His voice was carefully offhand.

She replaced the nozzle in the pump, wiped her hands carefully on a paper towel, and bent down to the car to accept the money from the driver.

"Figure it's my turn to apologize."

The car drove away. Kate found herself wishing

somebody else would pull up, her dad would appear, her mother would call—anything. She didn't know what to say.

"Bad idea, I guess," Mike muttered, as the silence lengthened. He turned to hoist himself back into the cab.

"No. Wait."

He checked himself. "Want to see what I've got?" His eyes lightened and a grin began at one corner of his mouth.

"Well. . . sure."

He loped around to the back of the truck and lowered the panel with a crash. There was something long and rectangular sitting in the bed of the truck, covered with a tarpaulin. There were also two large coolers in there, and a fair amount of water was sloshing out of them.

Mike's grin widened. He pulled the tarpaulin off. "A tavern the other side of town just folded. They had to get rid of all their stuff and they said I could have this if I'd truck it away."

"What is it?" she asked. "Looks like a glass coffin."

"A fish tank. And wait until you see the fish. They're in the coolers. Not your usual fish, that's for sure."

"Mike, a fish tank? That size? I don't know if Dad—"

"Where is he? Let's ask him. I got to get those fish out of the coolers pretty quick—they're too big to stay there very long."

Where was her father? Up over the garage, of course. Had been all day. Kate would rather be torn apart by wild horses than admit that to Mike, however.

"He's in town."

"Never mind. You could put it on that counter beside the worm refrigerator," Mike said. "Your dad wouldn't care. Probably think it's great."

Kate had doubts about that, but Mike steamed on. She'd never seen him so enthusiastic.

"Word gets around, you'll get people pouring in here just to look at the fish. Business will boom. Your dad couldn't object to that."

No telling what her dad could object to, Kate thought.

"Here," Mike went on, jumping up into the back of the truck. "Come on up and take a look at these guys."

Reluctantly, Kate climbed up and peered in, then jumped back, startled, as a fish almost leaped out of one of the coolers.

"Mike! They're huge! What in the world are they?"

"That big white one there, see? With the whisker sort of things? That's an African walking catfish."

Kate looked at him, eyebrows raised.

"I'm not kidding. That's what it's called."

"It walks?"

"Who knows? Anyway, the flat black one lying around on the bottom is a stingray. Honest to god stingray. Bet you've never seen one before. Name's Fred. You can feed him worms right from your fingers."

"You've got to be kidding. My fingers aren't going anywhere near that thing."

Mike laughed. "Chicken. That other one on the bottom, that's a peco-something-or-other. I've forgotten just what. He lies around eating junk and fish guck that falls on the bottom. Keeps the tank clean."

"Delightful."

The dark-striped fish that had almost leaped out of the cooler suddenly made a dash for a blunt-nosed gray one.

"That nasty one's a cichlid. Real fierce. They're freshwater fish, the guy said, but sometimes they can live in water that's not too salty. He seems to be doing all right, anyway."

"Sure doesn't seem to slow him down any."

"The one he's trying to boss around is a goby. Weird sort of face he's got, isn't it? Looks like somebody punched in his forehead."

"Maybe your cichlid did," Kate said.

"No, he just bites."

"Oh. Very reassuring."

"Here, look at this one in the other cooler. It's a little shark."

"*Sure* it is."

"Really."

A small, torpedo-shaped body twisted itself desperately around in the cramped space.

"Doesn't look too happy," Kate commented.

"That's why I've got to get them out quick. They none of them are. We've got to get them into the tank as soon as we can. We can fill it with the hose, and I've got all the stuff to make the water salty. Heater, too, light, everything. I'm telling you, Kate, this outfit is worth a pile of money. Your dad—he couldn't help but want it."

Angie wasn't even around to ask, not that she'd probably dare make a decision about it anyway. It was up to Kate. She hesitated. At that moment, the cichlid leaped again.

"Okay," she said. "I guess . . . ."

Mike vaulted out of the truck. "Got to get somebody to help us take the tank in. Even empty, it's really heavy. I was hoping your dad would be here."

At that moment Barney bicycled up.

"A body!" Mike exclaimed. "Just what we need."

Barney propped his bike up against a gas pump and walked over toward them.

"I don't think Barney's too strong," Kate began.

"Looks pretty wiry to me," Mike said.

Barney stopped in front of them. "Hi, Kate," he said. His eyes were on Mike.

"Hi, Barn. This is Mike. Mike Bridges, Barney Phillips." To her surprise, Barney's face had gone cold and closed. He eyed Mike with distrust.

"New around here, aren't you?"

"Not too new," Mike answered. His voice was carefully controlled. "Been around a while."

"Yeah? How long a while?"

"Long enough."

"Hey, Barn. We need some help. Look what we've got," Kate broke in with a nervous laugh. She wasn't sure just what was going on here.

"What is it?" Barney was still staring at Mike.

"A fish tank. It's pretty heavy. Can you help carry it in?"

"I guess."

"Great. Thanks," Kate said. "I'll go and get the counter cleared off." What was it with those two, anyway?

Kate had been wrong to think Barney wasn't strong.

"Wow," she gasped when they had finally wrestled the tank into place. "You been working out or something, Barney?"

He flushed. "Got weights at home."

To impress Melanie, no doubt. She suppressed a sarcastic comment.

It took most of the rest of the afternoon to set up and fill the tank and get the fish into it. When it was all ready and the lights were on, the three of them sat back to admire it. Kate had to admit it was pretty impressive. A couple of tourists came in as they were resting. The woman was so taken with the fish that they stayed for half an hour, just watching them and drinking coffee.

"Might as well eat while we're here," she said, finally, and they ordered toasted bacon, lettuce and tomato sandwiches and fries.

"See?" Mike crowed when they left. "Your business is going to take off."

"You guys don't need me anymore," Barney said. "I've got to go." He got to his feet, and Kate followed him.

"Who is that guy?" Barney asked as soon as they got out of earshot.

"What's the problem, Barney? You and he were as bristly with each other as a couple of tomcats all afternoon."

Barney shrugged. "I don't like him. Guess he doesn't like me back."

"But you just met him. How can you say that?"

"Where does he come from? What's he doing here?"

For a moment Kate was at a loss for an answer.

"He. . . . He works down to town with Jed. Picks worms for us." The words came out sounding defensive.

"In other words, he's just a drifter. I don't like it. You shouldn't have strangers like that around the place, especially when you're alone so much."

"Barney, he's okay. It's not like he's the one been doing the robberies or anything—" She stopped abruptly. Why in the world had she said that!

Barney leaped on her words. "How do you know? You don't know anything about him, do you?"

"I'm just sure. . . . He wouldn't do anything like that . . . ." There was a growing hollowness inside her. "Why should you care, anyway?" The words rushed out to cover her confusion. "Why should you worry about me? It's not like I'm Melanie Davis or anything."

Barney blushed a deep, painful red. "Melanie has nothing to do with it," he stuttered. "It's just—you're my friend. I care about you, that's all." He grabbed for his bike and pedaled off.

Kate looked after him.

"Your boyfriend didn't like me much, did he?"

Kate jumped. She hadn't heard Mike come up behind her.

"He's not my boyfriend," she snapped. "He just rides the bus with me. You're the one said yourself I don't have any friends, let alone boyfriends."

"Okay, okay. Don't bite my head off."

Involuntarily, Kate moved away from him. Whatever had possessed her to blurt that out about the robberies to Barney? And why did Barney dislike Mike so much?

"Guess I'd better be shoving off too."

Kate didn't answer; then, as he climbed into the truck and slammed the door, she got herself back under control.

"Thanks," she called after him. "For the fish, I mean."

Mike leaned out the window and flashed that grin at her. "My apology accepted, then?"

Kate felt a warmth rising through her body. She couldn't stop an answering smile. "Of course. Mine?"

"Sure thing." He waved, and drove off with a protesting screech of gears.

"I don't know, Kate," Angie fussed when she appeared later on. "I don't know what your dad's going to say about those fish."

But when Steve finally staggered in from the garage he was too drunk to notice anything.

Kate stayed down after her parents went to bed. She turned off all the lights except for the tank, then pulled a chair up in front of it. The fish swam easily. Even the cichlid seemed peaceful now. It was calming, watching them. She smiled to herself, remembering Mike's enthusiasm. Really, he was just like a kid sometimes.

Her father's anger the next day was tempered somewhat by a hangover of larger than usual proportions.

"Fool thing," he muttered, when he finally saw the tank. "Be more trouble than it's worth. You got to take care of it, Kate, and if it costs anything, out it goes."

"It won't cost much to feed them, Dad," Kate answered. "We've got the worms. Mike says it won't cost us much at all."

"That's another thing," Steve growled. "That kid, Mike. I don't think I want him hanging around here. The police were over at Jed's the other day, asking about him."

Kate froze. "What about him?"

"They were checking him out. Wanted to

know where he was the other night when that store got ripped off."

"He was at the fireworks," Kate said. "I saw him there."

"Store got robbed long after the fireworks were over. Could have been him easy."

"Dad! He wouldn't . . . ." The words petered out.

Luckily, Steve was in town the next time Mike turned up. He was driving Jed's pickup again, this time filled with lumber. Kate saw him from the window of the snack bar.

"Miss?" A plaintive voice came from one of the tables as she headed for the door. "My coffee?"

Kate appeared not to have heard.

"What are you doing back here so soon?" Her hand strayed to her hair and she tucked an errant strand behind her ear. She kept her words light with an effort; there was a battle going on inside her. Her father's words echoed in her mind, ominously, but she couldn't check the sudden flash of pleasure at seeing him. "What in the world have you got now? And how come you're not working today?"

"Got the day off. This was in that tavern's basement and they said I could have it too. Thought you might like a picnic table out to the side there. People could buy stuff and eat there when they stop for gas, you know? Lots of places have them, and that bit of field there, that would be perfect. What do you think?"

"Mike, you don't need to do this."

"Yeah. I know. But I figure—why not? Got nothing else to do. Besides—I owe you."

"Owe me? What for?"

"You know. Hadn't been for you—God knows where I'd be now."

"Oh, that." It was the last thing Kate wanted to think about. "Forget it."

"Well, anyway. I got the lumber here now. Might just as well make the table. Don't you want it?"

"Sure. It would be great." As long as her dad didn't turn up.

The pumps and the snack bar kept her busy all afternoon. Angie helped during the morning, but the lure of her soaps had been strong and now she was flopped out on the living-room couch with a Coke. By suppertime Kate was exhausted. Steve, luckily, had not turned up. She finished gassing up an overpowered convertible, handed the driver his change, and started back to the snack bar. The air conditioner was having fits again, but at least it was marginally cooler in there than out here on the shimmering tarmac. She reached a hand back to lift her sweat-soaked ponytail off her neck. She could certainly use a cold Coke too.

"Just a minute there, babe!"

She turned back to the car, bristling.

"You short-changed me, honey. Short a quarter."

Give me a break, Kate thought. The driver

was a man in his mid-thirties, dressed in the latest yuppie-fashion sports clothes, complete with designer sunglasses that must have cost more than she earned in a month.

"Well, *silly* me!" she drawled in her best Dolly Parton imitation. She reached into her pocket, pulled out two dimes and a nickel, and tossed them into the passenger side of the car.

"Have a nice day," she caroled, the words syrup-sweet.

"Hey!"

The last she saw of him before she turned away, he was scrabbling on the floor of the car, messing up the carefully pressed knees of his slacks.

Sounds of hammering had been going on all day, but Kate had only registered them in the back of her mind; she'd been too busy to pay much attention to what Mike was doing. When she finally dug her Coke out of the refrigerator, however, she became aware of a silence. She was just popping the top when he pushed through the door.

"Finished! And not bad, either. Come on outside and take a look." He was soaked in sweat, dark hair plastered to his head.

"You look hot. Want a Coke first? On the house."

"Sure. Thanks." He took the can from her, then threw himself down beside her. They watched the fish for a few moments in silence.

"Like them?" Mike asked.

"Yes," Kate answered. "I do, actually. I watched them for ages last night." Her voice turned dreamy. "I wonder what it would be like to swim in the ocean. You know—scuba dive in the tropics? Right down under the water there with the fish?"

The cool air from the air conditioner, slight though it was, felt good on the back of her neck. Stephanie, lounging on her tropical beach, rolled up again on the screen of Kate's mind. The cool air became a light ocean breeze. A tall, dark stranger, laden with scuba gear, was approaching her.

"You arranged for a diving trip, miss?" he asked. "We are ready now."

Stephanie donned the weight belt, tank, and buoyant, life-protecting vest. Mask, flippers—the water was so warm here only a light, close-fitting T-shirt was necessary over her bikini. She reached out her hand to her partner. Together, they walked into the foaming surf. The caressing water reached her knees, her thighs. A splash of spray suddenly drenched her and she cried out, but in delight.

"We swim now," the stranger said.

She let her body sink into the waves, lowered her masked face to the surface, and took her first look at the world below . . . .

eight

"We could plant some flowers along the wall," Mike said. "And the tree gives good shade. Too bad you only have an outhouse for customers, though. You sure your dad wouldn't let them use the bathroom in the house?"

Stephanie was abruptly erased, scuba gear and all. Kate got up to follow Mike outside. "Are you kidding?" she asked. "No way would he let anybody in there."

"It's a problem. People nowadays don't like that."

"As a problem, that's the least of my problems." Kate sat down on the picnic-table bench and winced as a splinter stabbed into her thigh.

"I'll get it all sanded down and then stain it," Mike said quickly.

Kate ran her hand over the rough surface. "You did a real good job, Mike. Thanks a lot."

Mike looked embarrassed. "No big deal," he said. "Like I said, I got nothing better to do anyway."

"You thought anything about what you're going to do this fall?" Kate asked, careful not to look at him. "I mean, like going home or back to school or anything? There won't be much here for you then."

He shrugged and tossed his hair out of his eyes with a flip of his head. "Face that when I come to it, I guess. Sure won't be going back to school. I've finished with all that. Going home . . . I can't do that."

"Why not?"

"Just can't." There was a finality about his voice that closed the topic. "Whatever happened to that house over there, by the way?" he asked, changing the subject. "You never did tell me." He gestured toward the burned-out foundation in the field next to them.

Kate stood up. She hadn't talked about the house to anybody since the fire. Most of the local people knew the story anyway and didn't bring it up.

Mike jumped to his feet as well. "I know," he said quickly. "Sorry. None of my business."

"No. It's okay. It's just . . . depressing, I guess." She traced the outline of a knothole on the picnic-table top. "It used to be our house. At least, it was going to be. Dad and Mom, they'd saved ever since they got married. Finally got enough to buy this place and build a house next to it. Dad was so enthusiastic about running his own business—he had so many plans. Going to make a really good restaurant, maybe a motel for truckers later on. The house was just about done—we were getting ready to move into it— but the wiring wasn't finished in the basement. Dad had a big fight with the guy who was doing it about how much he was charging us for it— finally kicked him off the place. Said he'd finish it himself. So he did, but the inspectors wouldn't approve it. Said it had to be done by a licensed electrician. Dad got mad at them too. He gets so mad sometimes. . . . Anyway, before we could move in, one night, there was a fire. There was nobody around—we lived in town at the time— and by the time somebody finally called the fire department, it was too late. The house was gone. Burned down right to the ground. Nothing left but what you can see now."

Kate raised her eyes to look at the ruin, but she wasn't seeing it. In her mind she was seeing a white frame house with green shutters. Gleaming, spotless kitchen, a living room with a light blue shag rug and an enormous stone fireplace, and her room. She'd decorated it herself. Forest green and burgundy.

"Wouldn't pink be prettier?" Angie had asked,

a little taken aback by the strong colors, but she'd insisted. Angie had done their bedroom up in a froth of flowers, fluffy curtains, and bows. Kate had thought her dad would hate it, but he'd just laughed and let Angie have her way. They'd hardly ever fought in those days. Angie had been so happy. Always smiling. That house had been their lifetime dream.

"Insurance?" Mike asked. He looked as if he knew the answer.

"Wouldn't cover it, of course. The wiring hadn't been approved, and they found out the fire was caused by an electrical malfunction. Something Dad had done wrong. We couldn't collect a cent. Everything they'd saved, everything they'd spent—and they'd gone into debt for the furniture and stuff—it was all gone. We're still paying it off."

"Your dad. . . . No wonder. . . ."

"He can't get over it. Blames himself."

"Hates himself too, I guess. I sure know about that."

Kate looked at Mike in surprise. His face had darkened.

"Yes. I guess he does. I never thought of it that way. We don't hate him for that—Mom and I. Not for that."

"The drinking?"

Kate didn't answer.

"Guess that's the only way out for him," Mike said. "Why doesn't he tear what's left down? Get rid of it?"

"Sometimes, when he's been drinking, he just sits and stares at it. Sometimes I think he cries."

The snack bar emptied early that night. Kate pulled out the notebook from under the counter, but she didn't start writing right away. Talking to Mike about the house—it had brought it all back. Most of the time, she just pushed the whole business out of her mind. It hurt too much to think of it. But Mike—funny how he seemed to understand things. It made her feel better. Almost unconsciously, she began to write.

Jed was tall, and probably wouldn't be considered handsome by most people, but there was something irresistibly attractive about him. He obviously worked outdoors a lot. He had dark, waving hair, in bad need of a haircut, that he kept tossing out of his eyes. It curled a little on the back of his neck in a way that made you want to reach out and touch it. His hands were strong and competent. You knew at once he would be good at building things. And his eyes—so blue! They crinkled a bit when he laughed, but that was not often. He looked as if he carried a secret deep within him. Sometimes he looked dangerous . . . .

It didn't occur to her she had just described Mike.

During the next two weeks there was another robbery at a local convenience store, and two others in nearby towns. People were starting to get in a turmoil. Kate herself, although she would never admit it, was beginning to feel nervous when she was alone in the evenings in the snack bar.

If it isn't Mike, then I'm in as much danger as anybody else, she caught herself thinking.

What do I mean, "if it isn't Mike"? Of course it isn't Mike. It could be anybody. One of the bikers. Somebody from out of town. There was a really crummy-looking guy in here just the other day, it could be him. If I really thought it was Mike, I would report it, wouldn't I? Of course I would.

But if it isn't Mike, then I *shouldn't* be alone so much. Maybe that crummy-looking guy was casing the place. Setting it up for his next hit ....

Her mind went back and forth like a ping-pong ball.

And she *was* often alone. Her father was drinking steadily again, not even trying to hide it. He spent more time in the room over the garage than anywhere else, and was rarely around to help out.

Melanie Davis and her gang drove up for gas the day after the third robbery. Kate winced at the thought of having to serve them, but she had no choice. They didn't pay her much attention, however.

"Oh, hi, Kate," the driver, Jerry Dunn—Melanie's latest conquest—threw out.

"Were you really there?" Mercy Harris, Melanie's best friend, was asking.

"I sure was!" Melanie skipped out of the car and over to the Coke machine. She dropped a coin in the slot and grabbed the can as it rolled down, then hopped back in. "I'd gone in after work and I was, like, in the corner? Looking through the magazines? I saw the whole thing. I don't think he saw me, though. It all happened so quick. Gus sure didn't hesitate about giving him the money, not after that other guy got cut."

"What did he look like?" Mercy sounded just about as awestruck as the Davidson boy.

"Couldn't tell. He had this mask thing over his face, you know? But there was something . . . ." She suddenly looked at Kate. Her face grew thoughtful. "There was *something* familiar about him, as if I'd seen him somewhere . . . ."

Kate fumbled Jerry's change. Jerry retrieved it just before it fell.

"Thanks, Kate." He dropped the gearshift into drive and peeled out, almost before the words were out of his mouth.

Mike turned up a few minutes later. Kate watched him swing down out of a truck he'd hitched a ride in and walk toward her. He'd been coming over more and more in his spare time lately—Angie had even mentioned what a help he was. Kate looked around. The stacks of useless old tires had disappeared, and the service station had begun to take on a tidy, more efficient look. Steve grumbled now and then at his being around, but never followed through.

"Coffee hot?" Mike called out as he came toward her, picking up a styrofoam container and pitching it in the trash barrel.

Acts like he owns the place, Kate thought with a sudden, irrational stab of annoyance. She watched him as he strode toward her. He moved so confidently. There was no mistaking that cocky walk.

At the same moment a police cruiser pulled in. Mike checked himself and suddenly turned away. The driver got out.

"Got any chocolate-covered doughnuts today, Kate?" the driver called.

It was Constable Downey; Kate knew him well. He strode over. Mike disappeared around the side of the building. Kate watched the officer come toward her. If she was going to tell anyone about Mike, he would be the one to choose. She'd known him for years. She trusted him.

But what if Mike *was* innocent and he arrested him? She'd be responsible for ruining Mike's life. He'd had a hard enough time of it already. Could she really do that to him?

She followed the constable into the snack bar, dumped two doughnuts into a bag, took his money and made change, responding to his jokes all the while, although she didn't have the slightest idea what she was saying. It was as if she were somewhere outside of herself, watching it all happen.

Constable Downey got back into the cruiser,

waved and drove off. When Mike reappeared he was almost determinedly casual. He didn't say why he'd suddenly lit out. Kate didn't have the nerve to ask.

She was just about to close up that night, long after Mike had left, when she heard a motorcycle roar into the station. She tensed. She hadn't seen her father since noon, and as far as she knew, her mother had gone to bed. The bikers came in fairly often and had never given her any real trouble yet, but she didn't feel up to facing one of them right now. It was too late. Besides— that young one, Rod, his name was, seemed to think trying to make time with the waitress was part of the image. The others kept him in line, but if that was him coming in now, she sure didn't want to have to deal with him on her own. Before she could make it to the door to lock it, however, it was pushed open. She dodged back.

A helmeted figure strode in, dressed in jeans and a leather jacket. No spider on it. Kate couldn't tell which one of them it was.

Then she took another incredulous look. He took off his helmet and leaned easily against the doorway.

"Barney!"

"Hi there, Kate." A futile attempt to be casual battled briefly with excitement, then lost. "I got it! Got it yesterday, and it's just about all paid for. Come on outside and look at it!"

"I don't believe it, Barney! The jacket—the helmet! I don't believe it!"

"Come on, Kate," Barney urged.

The black and red motorcycle from the dealership window stood shining in the gas-station lights.

"Isn't that the most beautiful thing you've ever seen?" Barney's voice was triumphant.

"It's . . . it's great," Kate agreed weakly. She was stunned. Seen this close up, it looked huge. No way could she imagine Barney on that. Suddenly she remembered Barney's father.

"What about your dad," she asked.

Barney's mouth thinned, "Don't ask," he said. "Don't even *ask*. Let's just say things aren't too happy at home right now. But this is one time I am *not* giving in. I bought it and I paid for it. It's none of his business." He shook his head as if to rid himself of the thought of his father, then his eyes lit up again. "Get your jacket, Kate. I'll take you for a ride."

"Oh, no. You're not getting me on that thing."

"Come on, Kate. You'll love it."

"Forget it, Barney. Anyway, I can't. Can't leave the snack bar."

"Close it up. It's almost closing time anyway and there's nobody here. You can shut up a little early. Come on, Kate—please?"

Kate wavered. She had never been on a motorcycle in her life—never wanted to be. Still, it *was* Barney. He was looking at her with such a pleading look—almost desperate. It obviously meant a lot to him.

"Oh, okay," she said finally. "I'm going to regret this, though, I just know it."

"No, you're not, Kate. I promise. You'll love it."

"Wait until I've got everything locked up," Kate answered, still dubious.

"I really don't want to do this," she repeated as she finally followed Barney over to the bike. He handed her a helmet and helped her put it on. It felt heavy and awkward.

"Sure you do," he insisted.

He obviously wasn't about to let her back out. Kate sighed in resignation.

"Don't go too fast, okay?" she said as she swung one leg over the seat and clung to Barney's waist. Her words came out muffled.

"Don't worry." He started the machine up. "Hold tight!" He swerved sharply out of the station and onto the highway with a deafening roar.

Kate felt her heart leap up into her throat and she closed her eyes in terror. Clutching onto Barney, she hunched down against him as close as she could. Why in the world had she ever agreed to this? She must be crazy. She felt the motorcycle wobble beneath her and she let out a cry that was immediately lost in all the noise. The wind whipped past them. Her hands were suddenly cold.

"Kate! Not that tight!" Barney shouted back over his shoulder. "I've only got one set of ribs."

Kate forced herself to loosen her grip, then grabbed hard again as Barney pulled out to pass a truck.

"Not so fast, Barney!" she shrieked. "Don't *pass* things!"

Barney didn't answer. After a few more moments, when nothing terrible seemed to have happened yet, Kate got up the nerve to raise her head and take a tentative peek over his shoulder. The road ahead of them was empty, the fields on either side dark. The motorcycle headlight cut a single beam through the blackness. Kate relaxed slightly. She had no idea how fast they were going, but there was no sensation of speed now. The motorcycle purred smoothly through the night.

Another couple of minutes, and she found she was actually beginning to enjoy herself. It was as if they were totally alone—the rest of the world, outside of this one narrow ribbon of road, didn't even exist. What if they just kept going on and on? What if they never stopped? Like the Flying Dutchman, sailing endlessly over the seas, alone for eternity. . . .

The headlights of an oncoming car suddenly rushed up at them and just as suddenly passed and left them in darkness again. Kate was shocked back into awareness, but the fear didn't return. She leaned against Barney easily, feeling the unexpected hardness of his muscles beneath the jacket. It felt reassuring.

They finally pulled back into the service station. Kate jumped off.

"You were right, Barn. It was fantastic. I mean it. Really fantastic! I had no idea it could be such fun."

"See? I told you, didn't I? I told you you'd love it." He turned to put their helmets back on the seat.

"Where the *hell* have you been?"

The words were loud and slurred.

"Dad!"

Her father was standing in the snack-bar doorway, swaying slightly.

"You little slut! Running around with motorcycle bums in the middle of the night!"

"Dad! It's Barney! I just went for a ride—"

"Close up the store early and head out, eh? Thought I wouldn't find out, didn't you? I'll teach you. I'll teach you what's right and what's wrong. No daughter of mine runs around with motorcycle bums."

Kate stared at her father in horror. She stumbled back against Barney.

"Get away from that scum!"

Steve lurched toward them, one arm upraised, fist menacing.

"Dad, you don't understand. It's not what you think."

"I know what I see!"

Before Kate realized what was happening, he opened his hand and brought it down hard against the side of her face. Her head rocked back. The force of the blow knocked her off her feet and sent her sprawling onto the cement. At the same moment Barney jumped forward, putting himself between her and her father.

"Leave her alone," he shouted.

"As for you," Steve began, and raised his arm again.

Barney charged. He aimed a blow with his right fist that Steve parried easily, but then swung with his left and landed a thudding punch to the older man's stomach. Steve hunched, gasping. Barney threw himself on him with a fury that carried both of them to the ground.

"Barney! Dad!" Kate screamed. She leaped to her feet and ran toward them. "Barney, stop!" she cried as Barney, in a frenzy of rage, punched and punched again at Steve.

He took no notice, then suddenly seemed to hear her. He stopped, shook his head slowly from side to side as if clearing it, then allowed Kate to pull him to his feet, away from Steve. Her father lay doubled up, choking. Kate started for him, panicked, but was brought up short when he started to retch.

"Get out of here," he panted finally. "Get the hell out of here, both of you."

Kate looked at her father lying on the ground, spattered with his own vomit. She felt something die within her.

nine

"Go, Barney!" Kate choked the words out, then turned and ran for the snack bar and her own room. As she threw herself down on her bed she heard the motorcycle thunder out of the station.

She was still there late the next morning when there was a tentative knock on her door.

"Kate? Kate, you've slept in. I need you downstairs."

Angie.

"Barney's here. Says he wants to see you. He's acting sort of strange. Kate—is anything wrong?"

"Tell him to go away." The vision of her father, drunk and raving, flooded back. Hot, sour shame turned her own stomach nauseous. She couldn't ever face Barney again.

"Why? What's the matter?" There was a sudden, unaccustomed sharpness to Angie's voice.

"Nothing. Just leave me alone."

Instead, Angie opened the door and came in. She was hesitant, but not in quite the same way as usual.

"Kate—did anything happen last night?"

As if she didn't know. How could she not know?

"Kate, answer me."

"No. Nothing happened." Kate turned to the wall, away from her mother's worried eyes.

"I heard your father yelling. He didn't come to bed last night. As far as I know he's still in that room over the garage. Did . . . did you have a fight?"

Kate stiffened. This was the first time Angie had ever said anything—ever brought anything out into the open. For a moment she hesitated, then closed herself off again.

"Nothing happened," she repeated.

"Then why won't you talk to Barney? What did he do?"

This wasn't like Angie at all, and there was no way Kate could deal with it right now. She wasn't ready for it. She had to stop it.

"All *right*. I'll go down. Tell him I'll be there in a minute." She swung her feet off the bed. Angie still didn't make a move to leave. "I said I'm going down, leave me alone, okay?" Instinctively, she put up a hand to cover her cheek. It hurt. Was there a bruise?

Angie's eyes followed her movement. They narrowed. Kate caught her breath.

But Angie didn't follow through. "Okay," she said, backing out the door. "I'll tell him."

Kate headed for the mirror. There was a bruise. After washing her face, she reached for the makeup she rarely bothered with and slathered it on. In the harsh daylight it looked heavy and fake, but it covered the discoloration. Her face looked gaunt, her eyes dark. There were puffy circles under them. She plastered on more makeup, then in desperation added a slash of bright lipstick. She looked like a clown. She rubbed off the lipstick, gritted her teeth so hard it sent a fresh splinter of pain up her already aching jaw, and went downstairs.

Barney looked as embarrassed as she was.

"Look—I'm really sorry. I mean . . . about what I did last night."

"It's not your fault." The words came out woodenly, all wrong.

"It's just, when I saw him hit you . . . ."

"He was drunk. He gets that way sometimes. Forget it, Barney."

"But if I hadn't been here none of it would have happened. If I hadn't made you go with me. . . . I feel like it's my fault, Kate."

"Don't be stupid!" Even more wrong. Kate tried to pull herself together, but she couldn't bring herself to look at him. "Of course it wasn't your fault."

Barney looked at her helplessly. "I always mess everything up. Just like my dad says. If there's an idiotic way to do something, I'll be sure to do it."

The smartest guy she knew? He had to be kidding. "Don't be dumb, Barney," she said. "Look, let's just forget about last night, okay?" She picked up a dishrag and started to wipe up a coffee ring on the counter.

Barney looked as if he wanted to say something else, but she forestalled him. She didn't want to hear anything more about his dad. She had problems enough of her own. "I'm sort of busy."

"I'll help if you like. I didn't bring the motorcycle. If your dad comes in I'll disappear fast, okay?"

"No. I don't need any help." Kate regretted the words the moment they were out of her mouth. They sounded cold and angry. She hadn't meant them that way. She probably should be thanking him. But how could she? Thank a guy for beating up on her own father? It was too much. The whole thing was just too much.

Barney dropped his eyes. "Yeah. I understand."

"Barney . . . ."

But it was too late. He was already out the door.

There was a commotion in the fish tank. The cichlid made an angry dash for Fred, and the stingray retreated under the gravel with an injured air about him. Kate stared after Barney, all kinds of feelings milling around inside her, not the least of which was guilt. She turned to the refrigerator and yanked open the door to get worms to feed the fish, fighting the feelings down. It wasn't fair. Why should *she* be the one to feel guilty?

She dumped the tub out onto an old board and took up a knife. Wielding it viciously, she sliced worms into slivers, for once not even noticing how disgusting the job was. Angie came in with a funny look on her face. She'd probably been listening to every word. Kate turned away and began to make a fresh pot of coffee.

"Look, Kate," Angie began.

"I've got a load of washing to do," Kate interrupted. "Be right back." She almost ran into the laundry room. She stayed there for as long as she dared, but when she heard a car draw up and honk for service, she knew she had to come out. Rather than go through the snack bar, she angled around the side of the house. It was a carload of fishermen, noisy and boisterous. They spilled out and into the snack bar. When she finished gassing up their car, Kate followed. Angie would never be able to cope with that lot.

Mercifully, the rest of the day was almost insanely busy. Not once was there a break long enough for Angie and Kate to talk. Kate was thankful for that. Several times she caught Angie looking at her with a more than usually worried expression on her face. It only added fuel to Kate's anger. Everything Angie did grated on her nerves today, but Angie, it seemed, was in a state of nerves even worse than Kate's. She bumped into things, spilled things, and dropped a trayful of glasses. They didn't mention Steve, or the fact that he hadn't come out all day, but Angie's eyes kept straying to the window and the garage beyond.

By closing time there was no avoiding the fact that there had been no sign of her father for almost twenty-four hours. As the last of the customers left and they hung the CLOSED sign on the door, Angie finally broke.

"I'm going over to that room, Kate. I've got to see if he's all right."

"Probably just passed out." The callousness in her own voice shocked Kate out of her anger for a moment, then she shrugged. As far as she was concerned, from now on she couldn't care less what her father did. Or her mother either, for that matter.

Ten minutes later Angie came back. All the frantic nervousness of the day was gone; she moved like an automaton. Her dress was torn, one eye was red and swelling fast, her lip was bleeding. She gave Kate a curiously blank look, then reached for the telephone.

"Mom! What happened?"

Staring at Kate as if she were a total stranger, Angie spoke into the receiver.

"Police? I want to report an assault. My husband—he's drunk. He beat me."

"Mom! What are you *doing*?"

Angie gave the address in a voice almost eerily calm. She hung up.

"Mom! You can't do that! You can't call the police on Dad!"

"I've had all I can take, Kate. And he hit *you* last night. He admitted it. Says he'll do it again if he has to. Says he's got to 'straighten you out'."

"He won't, Mom. Call them back. We can work it out . . . ."

"No. He's gone too far, Kate. This time he's finally gone too far. I kept waiting—hoping he'd change, straighten up—I can't fool myself any longer. It's not going to happen."

Kate lunged for the telephone; Angie put herself in front of it.

"No, Kate!" Her voice spiraled higher. "I won't let him hurt you again. I'm your mother! I can't let him do that!"

"I'll go talk to him . . . ."

"NO!" What was left of Angie's self-control finally shattered. "Don't go near there!" She grabbed Kate by the arm. "I mean it, Kate. I've never seen him like this. Don't go anywhere near him!"

A police car pulled up, siren screaming. Angie ran out. Kate saw her pointing at the garage door. Two officers began pounding on it, calling Steve's name. When there was no response, they opened it themselves and pushed through.

Kate watched as if she were watching something on TV. This couldn't be happening. This couldn't be real. Even when she saw them pull her father out of the room, filthy, stinking, staggering, and swearing—even when she heard Angie say, "Yes, I'll come with you and sign a complaint"—she couldn't make sense of it.

Angie turned back before she got into the police car.

"You'll be all right, Kate? I'll be back as soon as possible . . . ."

There was no room in Kate's throat for words. She was still sitting, alone and stunned, when Mike turned up.

"I heard," he said.

Kate looked at him. "She called the police on him," she whispered. "My mother. Called the police on him. On my father. Her own husband."

"About time, too, from what I've seen," Mike answered.

"But the police! You don't call the police on your own family!"

"You do if you want to live. What did you want her to do—wait until he killed her? Or you?"

"He wouldn't have—"

"Oh no? I suppose you got that bruise on your face by walking into one of your mother's doors?"

"You don't understand. You couldn't understand. Something like this can't happen to us!"

"Wake up, Kate, it just did. What makes you think you're so different from everybody else? Your mother's finally showing some guts, that's all."

"Guts?" Kate echoed the ugly word. "Is that what you call it?"

"You got to fight back in this world, Kate. You don't, you just get wasted." The words came out cold, flat, and hard.

The next morning Kate got up and went down to the snack bar as usual, but she left the CLOSED sign up. Angie had come back late the night before and had looked in on her before going to her own room, but Kate had pretended to be asleep. In reality, she hadn't slept at all. She sat now at the kitchen table, but made no effort to get herself anything to eat.

When Angie came down she paused in the doorway.

"I've got to go down to the jail, Kate," she said. "If your dad's sober they'll probably let him out until he goes before the judge." Her voice shook. She sounded frightened, as usual, but there was a determination about her that was new. "When he does, Kate, I'm still going to press charges."

"Why, Mom? Why are you doing this to us?"

"It's not me that's doing it, Kate. It's your father. And if I don't stop it, it's just going to happen over and over again." Angie came to the table and reached out for a chair. Her eye was an angry purple now, and almost swollen shut. Kate couldn't look at it.

"Try to understand, Kate. I have to do this.

He even hit you!"

"I don't care what he does. He can't hurt me."

"No. It has to stop," Angie repeated. She pressed both hands to her head. Kate could see her fingernails digging white grooves into her scalp; the scarlet polish on them was mostly peeled or gnawed off. "There was a doctor there last night, Kate. He said . . . he said it was because of the booze. He said that if your dad goes to jail he'll get treatment. He'll be made to go off the booze. He might get better."

"But in the meantime he knows he's going to go to jail. And if he's sober today, what's he going to say about that? What's he going to do? You know how mad he gets. What's to stop him from getting drunk again tonight, and what's going to happen then?" In spite of herself, Kate's voice trembled.

"I don't know." Angie's voice shook too.

"But you're still going to do it," Kate said.

"I'm still going to do it," Angie answered.

Kate shoved her chair back from the table and jumped to her feet. Angie's voice stopped her before she could reach the door.

"Kate—you can get out of here. Get into a university—you'll be out of here and gone. But I've got to stay. And I can't stay if it's going to go on like this."

"You could leave." The words were hollow, Kate knew it.

"I don't want to leave. I want to stay here. I

want it to be like it was before, and I'm going to do whatever it takes to make it that way. You don't understand, Kate."

Oh, I understand, all right, Kate thought. I understand that my father's going to jail and my mother's sending him there. I understand that I'll never be able to face anybody in this town again. I understand that things were bad enough before, but they're going to be ten times worse now, and I don't have a thing to say about it! There was a whirlpool of darkness closing in on her—she was sucked remorselessly, relentlessly into it.

Kate watched Angie go out an hour later. She kept the CLOSED sign up and ignored any cars that drove in, but found herself prowling restlessly from room to room. She even turned the TV on, but the faces and the noise they made didn't make any sense. She left it on anyway, just to avoid the silence. She watched the fish swimming endlessly back and forth, and felt as caged in as they. By noon she couldn't ignore the hunger gnawing at her, but she couldn't be bothered making a sandwich. She grabbed some chips and drank a Coke. The hunger was appeased, but now there was a hard, burning knot in her stomach.

Angie came back soon afterwards. She walked into the living room where Kate was sitting, staring sightlessly at the TV. Kate looked warily behind her, but there was no sign of Steve.

"Dad still sleeping it off?" she asked. Her voice wavered in spite of her effort to sound cool.

"No. They put him in the hospital. Last night after I left he passed out and he hasn't come out of it. He's really sick, Kate."

Kate heard the suppressed panic in her mother's voice, but she couldn't help the relief that flooded through her. Whether she blamed her mother or not for having him arrested, she hadn't realized just how frightened she had been of Steve coming back.

When Kate came down the next day, she found Angie already in the kitchen, having coffee. Her mother was dressed carefully, she had curled her hair and combed it back. Her nails were clean and neatly manicured.

"Where are you going?" Kate asked.

"To the hospital. To visit your dad."

"I don't get it. You're going to have him put in jail, but you're all dressed up to go visit him. How can you be so hypocritical?"

"I don't think he'll be well enough to talk to me—he might not even know I'm there—but I have to go. The doctor will be there too. He said he'd tell me about treatment."

"Why can't you just arrange for treatment without laying charges?" Kate didn't even try to control the anger in her voice. She'd forgotten just how afraid she'd been the day before. Or, if she hadn't actually forgotten, she was choosing not to remember.

"The doctor said the chances of him following through with the treatment on his own aren't very good, Kate, even if he agreed to it, and he might well not. It's for his sake, too, I'm doing this, Kate."

"Sure it is." Kate's mouth twisted.

"Don't you want him to get better?"

"I don't want a father in jail!"

The words hung in the air between them. Finally, Angie spoke.

"Do you want to come with me?"

"No."

"We could close for the day. You could talk to the doctor yourself."

"No."

She was gassing up a car when her mother pulled out in the old pickup.

The day of the hearing arrived. Steve was still weak, but able to attend it. Angie volunteered the information to Kate, her mouth tight. They hadn't spoken to each other any more than absolutely necessary in the past few days.

"I suppose you won't come to the hearing, either," Angie said as she poured herself a cup of coffee and drank it. The cup rattled in the saucer.

"No way." Just the thought of seeing her father standing up before a judge, all the eyes in the room staring at him, being led away by a police officer to jail. . . . Would they handcuff him? The thought of it made her sick.

She was serving lunch to some customers out at the picnic table when Angie came back. Kate dumped their food in front of them, then went into the snack bar. Angie wasn't there. Kate went on into their own kitchen. Angie was sitting at the table, staring straight ahead. She had made up especially carefully that morning, but her face was chalk white. Her lipstick had either worn off or been chewed off. She was dry-eyed, but her shoulders were shaking.

"Three months," she whispered. "They gave him three months because it was a first offense and I asked them to go easy on him. And because he agreed to go into treatment. He looked so sad, Kate. He said he was sorry. He said to tell you how sorry he was. And he looked old. For the first time—he looked so old. I can't bear it."

Kate felt the sting of sudden tears in her eyes. She turned away quickly.

"Mike said it was for the best. He said I'd done the right thing." Angie seemed to be talking to herself.

"Mike?" Kate whipped back around. "He was there?"

"Yes. He found out when the hearing was. He was with us. I was real surprised to see him there, but it helped."

Kate felt a surge of anger. What right did he have to butt in? It was none of his business.

No, it was *your* business, a small voice inside her head said. It was you who should have been there. Don't blame Mike just because you're feeling guilty again.

Two days later, Jed called up. Angie had gone to town; Kate answered the phone.

"You seen anything of Mike?" Jed asked. "He's disappeared. Just took off. Didn't even collect his pay."

Before Kate could collect herself enough to answer, Angie opened the kitchen door. Kate took one look at her mother's face and dropped the receiver.

"It's Melanie Davis," Angie said. "They found her body late last night down by the river. She's been murdered."

ten

"Melanie Davis? Murdered? That's not possible!"

"It's true," Angie answered. "I can't believe it myself."

"When? What happened?"

"Last night. She was supposed to come straight home from her job at the mall to babysit her little brother, but when she didn't turn up by ten o'clock, her parents started phoning her friends. Mercy Harris works with her at Woolworth's. She said they left together and she saw Melanie take the river road home the way she usually does."

Angie's voice caught. She paused for a moment. "I can't believe it," she repeated, as if to herself. "That lovely girl." Then she made an effort and went on. "That's where they found her. The police. Melanie's parents finally called them and they started a search for her."

"How . . . ?" Kate couldn't finish the question. Her mind refused to accept what her mother was telling her. She'd seen Melanie just a little while ago. Melanie was her own age. How could she be dead?

"She was hit. On the head."

Angie stopped again. She looked as if she was about to cry. "The police found her about midnight. She'd been dragged off the path a bit, behind some bushes—I guess in the dark nobody saw her there until they started looking." Her voice broke. "She lay there all that time. . . . Poor girl. All alone. . . ."

Kate started to shake. In her mind she could see Melanie darting out of the car to the Coke machine. Melanie had seen the person who'd robbed the last store. She'd said there was something familiar about him. Had she realized who he was? Had he found out somehow? And that look she'd given Kate—what did that mean? As if . . . as if he had something to do with Kate.

And Mike had disappeared.

"Poor girl," Angie said again. "First those robberies, now this. What's happening around here?"

Angie wasn't the only one who started making connections between the robberies and the killing. The next morning two police officers strode through the door into the snack bar. One was Kate's friend, Constable Downey; the other was a new officer, one she hadn't seen before.

"Morning, Kate," Constable Downey said. His face was serious and the usual bantering tone in his voice was gone. "Your mom around?"

Angie came out of the back room, wiping her hands on a tea towel. Kate sidled back toward the counter. There was a sick uneasiness growing in her stomach.

"What is it?" Angie asked, her voice shrill. "My husband? Has something happened?"

"No, ma'am," the constable replied. "Nothing to do with Steve at all. We just want to ask you and Kate a few questions, that's all." His voice was studiously calm, but he looked ill at ease.

"Questions?" Kate went rigid.

"Yes." He looked over at Kate, then back at Angie. "You have a boy working here—name of Mike Bridges?"

"Yes," Angie answered, puzzled.

"He around here now, by any chance?"

"No," Angie answered. "He's probably up at Jed's. He works for him, mostly. Only helps out here now and then."

"Not anymore, he doesn't work there." The other officer spoke up for the first time. His voice was cold and unfriendly. Suspicious. "Seems he just took off somewhere in a big hurry. Nobody seems to know where."

"Why, I didn't know that," Angie said. "Did you, Kate?"

To her horror, Kate saw her hands start to tremble. The cup and saucer she was carrying suddenly clattered. She dumped them into the sink and clasped her fingers tightly together behind her back.

Angie jumped at the crash. Both officers' eyes swiveled to stare at Kate. She took a deep breath and forced the tremble out of her voice.

"Well—yes, actually. Jed called up yesterday and asked if I knew where he was. You came in with the news about Melanie then, Mom, and I guess . . . I guess I just forgot to tell you," she finished weakly.

"Did you have any idea he was planning on going anywhere?" the second officer asked.

"No. Not at all. The last time I saw him he seemed just the same as always—said he'd see me this week." Kate stopped abruptly. The officer furrowed his brow. He pulled out a memo book and started making notes.

"So you think he must have left in pretty much of a hurry, then—hadn't planned on it?"

"I didn't say that. I don't know . . . ."

"Know where he comes from?"

"Not really. Some little town near Ottawa, he said." The useless air conditioner roared in Kate's ears. She wiped a trickle of sweat off her forehead. "He never told me the name. Said I probably wouldn't have ever heard of it." Kate twisted her fingers together. A ring on her right hand dug into the flesh painfully.

"When did he first turn up here, Kate?" Constable Downey asked. His voice was quiet and kind. Kate turned to him with relief.

"In June it was, wasn't it, Kate?" Angie answered, before she could say anything. "Early June. Just before school let out."

The second officer made a note and nodded his head, as if confirming a thought. "Just before the first robbery—the one at the drugstore."

"Why, yes," Angie agreed, then her eyes widened. "But you don't think—"

"Just checking, Mrs. Halston," Constable Downey put in quickly. "We don't have any reason at all to suspect him, but it's sort of a coincidence, him arriving out of nowhere just before a string of robberies starts, then disappearing back into nowhere right after the first murder we've had in this town in over twenty years. Something we've got to check out. What did you think of him, Mrs. Halston?"

"Why . . . ." Angie was confused. "Why, he's a real nice boy. He's helped out a lot here. Even came to court with me when my husband . . . ." She bit her lip.

He turned to Kate. She felt as if she were fighting for breath in the heavy, humid air.

"What about you, Kate? What did you think of him? Anything strike you as unusual?"

"Unusual?" she parroted, stalling for time.

"Yes. Strange. Out of the ordinary." The constable looked at her closely. She wiped the sweat out of her eyes again.

Tell him about the first time he'd broken in here? About the attempted robbery? It was now or never. Her eyes slid away from his. There was a splash from the fish tank. The cichlid was harassing Fred.

"Kate?" Constable Downey repeated, gently prodding. His eyes drilled into her.

"No," Kate said. "Nothing. Nothing unusual."

"You're sure, Kate? There's nothing more you want to tell me?"

The constable's voice was so friendly. So reassuring. For a moment Kate weakened. It would be such a relief to tell him. To get rid of her secret and her fear. Let somebody else handle it. Let somebody else decide whether Mike was guilty or not. She opened her mouth.

"You keeping anything back from us, miss?" The second officer's voice broke in harshly.

"No!"

There was a moment of silence. Constable Downey glared at his partner, then he spoke again.

"You'll let us know, Kate? If you remember anything?" His voice was flat. He sounded disappointed. Kate was certain he didn't believe her. After a few more general questions they finally left.

"Kate, you weren't lying to them, were you?" Angie was looking at Kate strangely.

"Of course not!" She stumbled back behind the counter and made a show of collecting some dirty dishes, but they rattled so badly in her hands that she stopped and just grabbed onto the edge of the sink.

"I like Mike. I'm sure he didn't have anything to do with this," Angie said, "but it sure is funny, him taking off like that. If you do know something. . . . You've got to tell them, Kate. You can't hold things back from the police."

"You know all about that, don't you!" Kate exploded. "You certainly do know about telling everything to the police, don't you!"

Angie's face went cold. She threw down the towel she'd been holding and left the room.

The church where Melanie's funeral was held was far too small for the number of people who turned up to say goodbye to her. All of her high school friends and teachers were there, her relatives, her neighbors, her family's friends, even people who hadn't known her. The whole town grieved for her, and the whole town was shocked. Nothing like this had ever happened here before. She had been killed with a single blow to the head. With a blunt instrument, the police said. Swung by someone standing directly in front of her.

So she had been facing her killer. Had she had time to be afraid? Kate couldn't get the picture out of her mind.

Kate and Angie went to the funeral together, but they didn't speak much to each other. Since the day of the police officers' visit, Angie had seemed to withdraw into herself. She had been to visit Steve, but when she came home she went straight to her room without saying anything to Kate. Kate told herself she didn't care. She told herself she preferred it that way.

At first Kate didn't notice anything wrong at the church. She and Angie got there early enough to find places toward the back. Several of Melanie's friends were in the same row; they glanced at Kate and Angie, but didn't speak. When the church emptied, however, and the mourners began the short walk to the cemetery, following the hearse and the cars bearing Melanie's family, Mercy Harris fell into step beside Kate. Mercy's eyes were red and swollen from weeping. Three other girls and Jerry Dunn walked beside her.

"Police find your scummy boyfriend yet?" Mercy hissed.

Kate looked at her, dumbfounded. For a moment she thought she hadn't heard correctly.

"That lowlife—the one you've been so tight with all summer—the one that just disappeared so conveniently—they find him yet?"

"Police have been asking about him all over town. Seems the only ones know anything about him are you and Jed, and everyone knows Jed's not running on all cylinders," Jerry said. "Guess that just leaves you, doesn't it?" He raised his eyebrows; his words were heavy with insinuation.

"Pretty funny, him just disappearing like that. And nobody from around here had any reason to kill Melanie, that's for sure," Mercy said bitterly.

"You don't know what you're saying," Kate began, but they turned away and left her standing there. Kate fought to catch her breath. It took several moments to pull herself into any semblance of normality and catch up to her mother. Angie was staring at the cars ahead of them, however, and didn't seem to notice.

As they prepared to leave the cemetery after the brief ceremony, Kate caught sight of Barney. He was standing back, alone and a little apart from the rest of the mourners. His face was desolate. He looked up and saw her at the same moment, but before she could do anything, he turned brusquely and strode away.

Barney too? Kate thought in despair. He's blaming me too? He never trusted Mike right from the beginning . . . .

July melted into August. It was the hottest summer on record, the TV forecasters said. The air conditioner was fixed, but it still didn't work properly.

"Hotter'n you know what," Bob Dowles said, as he and the other three regulars settled down around their table one day not long after the funeral. There was still nothing new with the investigation; the townspeople were beginning to get angry. And frightened. Girls weren't walking home alone anymore, and everyone avoided the river road after dark.

"How's Steve?" Norris Lamont asked Angie, as she brought them their order.

"He's getting on real well," she answered with the brief flash of a smile. "Go to see him every week, you know. Sends you all his regards."

"Glad to hear it," Jimmy Bent said.

"He's making an effort, he really is. Time he comes home, he's going to be all better. Right back to the old Steve." She looked over at Kate, behind the counter.

Kate pretended not to hear. Angie had been after her to go with her to visit Steve, but Kate continued to refuse. She wouldn't even listen to her stupidly optimistic reports. Her father wouldn't be home by the time school started; how they would manage the station and the snack bar then she didn't know. There was one thing and one thing only she was sure of—she would not drop out of school to help out. No matter how bad things got. School was her only way out of this place. Her only escape.

But Barney—her one friend—hadn't come around again. He wouldn't be there for her at school either, she supposed. Remembering his face the day of the funeral, she couldn't blame him. And underlying everything else, lurking in the back of her mind all the time, was the question she couldn't avoid: did Mike do it? If he did, by not telling on him, was she responsible? Was she responsible for Melanie's death?

The snack-bar door slammed open, breaking into her thoughts. The young biker, Rod, stumbled in, closely followed by the older one, Bud. Rod tripped on the doorsill, then crashed into a chair and knocked it over. Conversation in the snack bar ceased, and all eyes focused on him. There was an audible grunt of disapproval from Bob Dowles.

"Drunk, looks like," he said, just loudly enough to be heard.

Rod glared at him and raised a fist, but Bud restrained him.

"Hey, guy. Sit down. Chill out, man." He looked up and saw Kate. "Can we have a couple of Cokes here, Kate?" he called out.

Kate put them on a tray and approached the table warily. When she got closer she could see half-healed scratches all down the side of the young biker's face. Bud saw her looking at them.

"Fight with his girlfriend," he said, laughing. "Kid's got a mouth on him that never stops. Guess you know that. He's a little the worse for wear today—she dumped him and he's taking it hard. Cut him some slack, okay?"

The boy didn't seem to be in any shape to give her trouble, but Kate avoided going around to his side of the table anyway. He was a real weirdo. For all she knew, he could be the killer. She caught her breath and stared at him. He *could* be the killer. Could have done the robberies too. He was just strange enough . . . .

You're clutching at straws, Kate, she told herself grimly. Just because he's a biker and you don't like him. Still, she kept well out of reach of his grubby paws.

"You going to come over and test drive a bike?" Bud went on, still laughing.

"Not likely," Kate answered, trying to keep her voice light. He was only teasing, she knew that, but her nerves were raw. She took the money for the Cokes, made change, and headed for their own kitchen.

"Kate?"

Angie's voice floated after her, but she kept on going.

eleven

Labor Day weekend was looming up; the blistering heat wave still hung on. Kate came down to open the snack bar and by the time she had put the coffee on she was already dripping sweat. She sank down behind the counter and dropped her head into her hands. Her notebook was stashed under there, but she ignored it. She hadn't written anything since Melanie's death. The way she felt now, she wasn't sure she would ever write anything again, and she didn't care. The police had been back, still asking questions about Mike. The only consolation was that if they were still asking about him, they still hadn't found him. But was that really so much of a consolation? If they found him, maybe he could clear himself. But then again, maybe he couldn't.

She didn't hear the bus stop outside; the door opening startled her. She looked up and there, as if he had stepped out of her thoughts, was Mike. It was so much like the first time she had seen him that for a moment she didn't even notice the girl standing beside him.

The girl was blond, her long hair straggly and unkempt, as if she hadn't yet had time to comb it this morning. Dark roots showed at the part. She was wearing a thin, crumpled white dress. A shiny black jacket, probably Mike's, was draped over her shoulders, crushing an already wilting, sad little corsage of deep red roses. She looked wan and tired.

The swing door opened and Angie swept in with a tray of sandwiches, then stopped dead.

"Mike!"

Mike grinned. A flustered, sheepish grin. A grin that Kate had never seen on him before. Then he put his arm around the girl. Pride, defiance, embarrassment, all seemed to be fighting to get the better of him. The girl leaned her head against his shoulder. She looked just plain scared.

"Mrs. Halston, Kate, this is Stacy."

"Stacy?" Kate managed to get out.

"My girlfriend from back home." He paused for a moment, looked down at the girl, and his grin widened. "I guess I mean—my wife. We were married yesterday. We've been on buses all night."

"Your wife!" Kate felt suddenly hollow. She flinched as if she'd been struck. She stared at Mike, but he wasn't even looking at her. All his attention was fixed on Stacy.

Angie was the first to recover.

"On buses all night? No wonder you both look so beat, you poor things. Sit down. I'll get you coffee and some breakfast." She bustled around behind the counter.

Mike led Stacy over to a table.

"Thanks," she said, her voice so low Kate could hardly hear her. "That would be really great, Mrs. Halston."

Kate stared at her. She was trying to remember what Mike had said about her.

Mike finally turned to Kate. "I guess I got some explaining to do," he said.

Kate could only manage a nod.

"I'm really sorry I took off like that. Without letting you know or anything. It was just—this came up so quick."

"What? What came up so quick?"

"I'd been thinking about Stacy more and more. All the time, actually," Mike said. "Worrying about her, you know?"

No, I don't know, Kate raged silently. You never said anything. Or hardly anything . . . .

"We'd had a fight. A really bad one. My fault. I thought she was pushing me too much—to get a job, go back to school—I just got fed up and left. Just wanted to get away from everything—my mom, Stacy blaming me for being such a loser—"

"I didn't, Mike," Stacy cut in.

"Yeah. I know. I was just being a jerk." He put a hand on her shoulder. She reached up to cover it with her own.

Kate winced at the sight of the narrow gold band on Stacy's finger.

"Anyway, I thought I could just leave—walk away and forget her—but I couldn't. I tried to pretend it was okay, but the longer I was away, the worse I felt and the worse it got. Finally it was so bad I couldn't stand it any longer and I phoned her up. That's when she told me. She wasn't going to, but I could tell something was wrong—something more than just the fight— and I made her."

"Told you?"

"She's pregnant. She hadn't told her parents or anybody yet. Hadn't even gone to a doctor. She was too scared. I knew I had to get back and help her, so I just hopped the first bus out."

Angie took two cups of coffee over to the table. She put them down, then gave Stacy a pat.

"I'll get you a bowl of cereal and some milk, honey, that's what you need. Either of you want some bacon and eggs too?" she asked.

Mike flashed another grin. "Thanks. I sure do. Didn't realize how hungry I was."

"Not for me, thanks," Stacy put in quickly. "Cereal would be just fine." She made a small grimace. "Seems I'm beginning to find out what morning sickness is all about." She put a tentative hand on her stomach and looked up at Mike. There was a world of love in the look. Then she looked back at Angie. "Let me help you get it," she added, and went to stand up, but Angie pushed her down gently.

"You just sit right there," she said.

Kate's mind was in a turmoil. What had Mike done? The idiot! Any chance he might have ever had to do anything with his life . . . .

"We went to a doctor, got Stacy checked out. Then we told her parents." Mike's face turned grim. "Her dad just threw her out. There wasn't anything we could say, anything her mom could say. Not that she had anything to say that we wanted to hear, anyway. She never did like me." His grip tightened on Stacy's shoulder. "We figured. . . we figured we'd just face this and get through it somehow. I've got that room down at Jed's, and work there for a couple more weeks, anyhow, then I'll just have to find something else. We'll make out. I'm sure we will." For the first time, his voice faltered.

"You certainly won't go back to Jed's." They all looked at Angie in surprise. "It seems to me you two are the answer to our prayers. With Steve gone for now, and Kate going back to school soon, I was at my wit's end trying to figure out how we'd manage. How about helping us out here? We can't pay you much, leastways not right now, but we'll give you what we can.

We can even fix up that room over the garage for you."

Kate stared at her mother as if a stranger had suddenly walked in and taken Angie over. This was *Angie* talking? *Angie* taking control and ordering everyone around? And she was offering Mike and Stacy a place here? To *live* here?

Mike's whole face lightened. "Do you mean it?"

"Of course I do."

"I've got experience," Stacy put in. "I've waitressed lots of places."

Mike grinned. The old, familiar grin. To Kate, it felt as if someone was twisting a knife inside her.

"That's the first good thing that's happened to us since this whole thing started. Mrs. Halston, what can I say? Thanks. Just—thanks!"

"Nonsense. I'll probably end up thanking you."

Angie fussed over Stacy until she finished eating, then hurried her out of the snack bar. "Stacy, honey," she said, "you come with me and we'll see about fixing up that room. Then you are going to lie down and take a good rest. You've got to take care of yourself."

"But I want to help." Stacy smiled, and her face looked suddenly pretty. And very young.

"You will," she said. "Oh, you will. I'll run you off your feet, depend upon it. But first you're going to rest." She threw a meaningful look at Kate. "Kate—you'd better bring Mike up to date on what's been going on around here."

The murder! Things had happened so fast

she'd forgotten all about that! The police were going to be after Mike as soon as they found out he was back.

Angie put an arm around Stacy's waist and led her out the door. Mike looked at Kate curiously.

"Anything wrong, Kate?" he asked.

"You haven't heard—what happened here?"

"I've hardly seen a paper or watched TV since I left. Too much else going on."

"Melanie Davis. She was murdered. No one knows who did it or why, but the police were around here asking after you."

"Me? Why me? I don't even know her."

"I know. It's just—the robberies happened right after you came. Melanie was in one of the stores that got robbed and was telling people she thought she might know who did it. Then you left right after she was killed. . . . People are talking, that's all."

"The police were around *here*?"

"Yes."

"What did you tell them?"

"The truth. I didn't know where you were. I didn't know why you'd gone, but I didn't think it had anything to do with anything that had happened here."

"Did they believe you?"

"I don't know."

"People—other people are talking too?"

"Some of Melanie's friends. They said something at the funeral." Kate half turned and began to straighten things on the shelves behind the counter.

"What about you? What do you believe?"

"Oh, Mike—of course I don't think you did it. Of course I don't." But she couldn't quite face him. A throbbing began behind her eyes. She reached a hand up to rub at her forehead.

"You sure?"

"I said so, didn't I?"

"Sounds like maybe you're not." Mike's face hardened. "Why should you be? After all, the first time you met me, I was trying to rob you. I threatened you. You tell the police that?"

Kate whirled around. "Of course not!"

"Why not?"

"They didn't ask. At least . . . ."

"But you are wondering, aren't you? You are worrying?" His voice was soft. His eyes had gone dangerous again.

"No! I'm not!" Then—she tried to stop herself, but couldn't—"Mike, *did* you have a knife that day?"

"Yeah, actually, I did. So what do you think now?"

Kate drew in her breath with a ragged, painful gasp.

"Guess you'll just have to wonder a bit more, won't you? If I did do it, I'm sure not going to confess now, am I?"

"Mike—"

"I'm going to see Stacy," he said. He turned and pushed his way out the door.

They came back in, together, just before noon. Angie and Kate were rushing, trying to serve two carloads of tourists. Mike carefully avoided looking at Kate.

"I'll take care of the gas pumps now, Mrs. Halston," he said. "Stacy'll help in here."

"Oh, Stacy, you should take it easy today," Angie protested.

"No way, Mrs. Halston," Stacy answered. She looked as if she had rested, and showered in the portable stall shower that was set up in the garage. Her hair was shining and pulled back in a ponytail. She had changed into jeans and a T-shirt. "I'm just fine. I'd like to start right away. What do you want me to do first?"

Kate dropped her dishcloth. "Be back in a sec," she said. She followed Mike out to the gas pumps.

"Mike, we've got to talk. What are you going to do?"

"I didn't tell Stacy anything. I don't want to worry her," Mike answered.

Stacy! Couldn't he think of anything except her?

"She'll find out. The police will come around again as soon as they hear you're back."

"I'll tell her tonight. I'd appreciate it if you didn't say anything to her first." The words were cold and formal.

"Of course I won't."

A car pulled in; Mike turned his back on her and went over to service it. Just then another car passing by on the road caught Kate's eye. It was Jerry's. It slowed down abruptly—Mercy's face was at the passenger window, staring at Mike. Then, just as suddenly as he had braked, Jerry put on the gas and sped away.

The day was a long, drawn-out hell for Kate. In spite of clouds that had been threatening all day, and the fact that the forecasters had promised a break in the heat wave, the weather was heavier and more sweltering than ever. It weighed Kate down to the point where she could barely move. There was an electricity in the air that set her nerves on edge. Stacy and Mike joked and laughed as if they hadn't a care in the world. Even knowing what he did, Mike acted as if they were on some kind of honeymoon. Every time Stacy walked by, he reached out to hug her, pat her or stroke her hair. Kate couldn't bear to watch them, couldn't bear to take her eyes away from them. She'd never known anything could hurt so much.

Ten minutes before closing time they heard the deep, muffled growl of a powerful car pulling up. Kate had just had time to register it as a police car when the door opened and Constable Downey walked in, closely followed by his partner. Ignoring Kate, he strode over to where Mike was standing beside Stacy, helping her clear a table.

"You Mike Bridges?" the constable asked.

Mike paled. He looked around quickly, casting his eyes from side to side as if considering making a run for it.

"Are you Mike Bridges?" Constable Downey repeated.

"Mike? What's going on?" Stacy's eyes were wide—startled.

"Yes." Mike forced the word out. He stayed where he was, but threw one arm out instinctively in front of Stacy.

"We'd like you to come with us down to the station, if you would, sir." Constable Downey's words were measured and polite.

"What for?"

"Just to answer a few questions."

"And if I don't want to go?" The words were belligerent, but they rang hollow.

"We don't want any trouble now," the constable said calmly. "It will just be for a while. Clear up a few things for us."

"You can ask me anything you want right here!"

"Listen, kid—" the second officer made as if to grab Mike's arm. Constable Downey moved in between, forestalling him. He sent the younger officer a warning glance.

"Mike, what *is* it?" Stacy had turned as white as Mike.

"Constable Downey, what grounds do you have? What makes you think . . . ?" Angie started out bravely, but floundered. Her words petered out.

The constable turned to Kate. "I've got a real suspicion you know more than you've told us, Kate. I'd like to talk to you again tomorrow, and

I suggest you do some serious thinking tonight."

Kate couldn't answer. How had they known Mike was back? Then the answer hit her. Mercy and Jerry, of course.

Mike turned to Stacy. His eyes were desperate.

"It's okay. Everything's going to be okay. Don't worry. Something happened here—I was going to tell you later. But I haven't done anything. Honest! I'll be back in a couple of hours. I haven't done anything, Stacy!" he repeated, then he turned back to Constable Downey.

"Okay," he said. "I'll go with you." He brushed off the second officer's hand as the man tried to grip his elbow, and strode past him. At the door he stopped and shot Kate a glance. His face was carefully blank, but his eyes held a mute appeal. She knew what he was asking.

The door slammed behind them. There was a sudden, unbelieving silence, then Stacy screamed.

"No!" She made a dash after them. "They can't! They can't take him!"

Angie caught her.

"Stacy! Stop!"

"But they're taking him to jail! What are they going to do with him?"

"They're not taking him to jail. They're just going to ask him some questions. Sit down, Stacy. Remember the baby! You're going to hurt yourself!"

"But why? What's going on?"

"Something happened. Just before he left."
Angie was talking feverishly, trying to make
Stacy sit down, but Stacy pulled away from her.

"What happened?"

Angie looked helplessly at Kate, but Kate just
shook her head. She was frozen inside and out.
Incapable of thought, let alone speech.

"A girl," Angie said finally. "Melanie Davis.
She was. . . she was murdered."

"Murdered! And they think Mike did it? Why?"

"There were some robberies too. Just after
Mike came here. Melanie saw the robber once.
He was disguised, but they think she might have
recognized him." Angie looked at Kate again,
frantic for help.

"Mike wouldn't do that. He *couldn't* do that!"
Stacy turned to Kate. "You know him. You know
he wouldn't hurt anybody. He told me about
you. Said you were a really great person. Said
you'd helped him a lot. You know he wouldn't
rob a store or hurt anybody, *don't you?"*

The image of Mike, sick and hungry, flashed
into Kate's mind. And he *had* had a knife. He'd
admitted it.

Kate stared back at Stacy. Then she turned
away and escaped through the swinging door
into the kitchen.

She stayed there, staring at the wall, while she
heard Angie calming Stacy down. Finally, she
heard Angie take Stacy out. She heard Angie

come back, heard sounds of crockery rattling.

"I'm going to take Stacy a cup of hot chocolate and sit with her for a while." Angie's head poked through the door. "Are you okay?"

"Yes."

A pause, as if Angie wanted to ask something further, then her head disappeared. Kate heard the snack-bar door slam.

Angie had probably forgotten to put the CLOSED sign up. The last thing they needed was for somebody else to come in now. Woodenly, Kate got up and went into the snack bar. Sure enough, the sign hadn't been switched. She headed for the door.

A clap of thunder shocked through the air. At the same moment, Kate heard the wind howl and a lashing of rain hit the windows. The door crashed open before she could reach it.

A helmeted figure strode in, drops of water beading and glistening off the blackness of his leather motorcycle jacket.

twelve

Kate froze in terror. The figure tore his helmet off.

"Barney!" Relief flooded through her. Her knees suddenly melted and she reached out to a table for support. "Oh, Barn! You don't know how good it is to see you . . . ." Her words trailed off. Barney's face was distorted—savage.

"He's back, isn't he?"

"Barney—what's wrong?"

"That guy—Mike. I just heard. He's back. And the police have arrested him."

"They've just taken him in for questioning. They said—"

"Why didn't he stay away?" Barney rushed forward and grabbed Kate by the arms. "Why didn't he just vanish? As long as they couldn't find him, everything was fine!"

"Barney, what are you talking about? Let me go! You're hurting me, Barney!"

He shook her, then threw her aside so violently she stumbled and almost fell. Kate looked at him unbelievingly. Barney?

He paced across the room.

"It wasn't my fault. It was an accident. As long as nobody else got caught for it, it was okay. It was an accident, Kate!"

Kate felt as if her heart were trying to burst out of her chest. Her mouth went dry.

"You went for a ride on my motorcycle with me, didn't you?" Barney exploded. "You didn't want to go, but when you did, you liked it, didn't you? You said you did."

She shook her head, helplessly. The motorcycle? What did that have to do with all this?

"It's so great, Kate, that motorcycle. Isn't it? You said so yourself. I knew, if I had that. . . things would change, Kate. No more Barney the nerd. Anybody who owned that would have power, Kate, wouldn't he? Girls wouldn't laugh at him then, would they?"

"Barney." It was the barest of whispers. "What are you saying?"

"And I had to do terrible things to get it, Kate." Barney paced back. "It's not easy to rob a store. It's scary. Your heart runs away with you, you're sure you're going to get caught. It takes guts to do that, Kate. My dad says I don't have guts." Incredibly, he laughed. "What would he say about that if he knew? What would he say about *that*? I even hurt somebody. I didn't mean to, but I did."

Kate reached behind her for a chair, put it between her and Barney.

"Your dad," he went on, slashing at the air with his fist as if slashing at an invisible enemy. "Your dad—sure he gets drunk. He hits your mom, he even hit you. I wish my dad would hit me. I could hit back then, same as I did with your dad. But your dad, it's the booze makes him do that. He really does love you. You know that. My dad—he hates me."

"No, Barn . . . ."

"*Yes!* All my life. Everything I've ever done. It's always wrong, or dumb, or stupid. You even said so yourself. 'Don't be dumb, Barn,' you said. 'Don't be stupid.' That's just what I am and he never lets me forget it. But I got away with those robberies, didn't I? And Melanie. Nobody suspects me. What would he say if he knew that?"

"Barney . . . ." This wasn't possible. It couldn't be happening.

He flung himself toward her and she cringed back.

"And my mom! Whenever he starts in on me she leaps in and goes at him. But it's not really for my sake. She just wants to hurt him. She goes at him and he gets back at her and pretty soon the two of them are saying the worst things they can to each other. It's like they hate each other so much they're trying to kill each other with words. And they've both forgotten me. They couldn't care less about *me*."

"Barney, that's not true. That can't be true . . . ." Kate faced him, turning with him as he started his frantic prowling around the room again.

Barney stopped as suddenly as if he'd run into a wall. He turned back toward Kate. His face looked as if it were falling apart.

"I waited for her. I knew when she finished work. I just wanted to offer her a ride home." His voice began to rise. "That was all—just one ride! Why wouldn't she want to ride on that motorcycle—even if it was only with me? How could she say no? But she did. She laughed at me. Said I looked like a fool riding around on it. Said everybody was laughing at me. I'd pretended there was something wrong with the wheel and I was fixing it. You know? Like, to have an excuse for stopping there. I was pretending to tighten a lug nut and I had this wrench in my hand. When she laughed. . . . Kate, you've got to believe me. I didn't mean to do it!"

"Barney, stop. Please. Stop." Kate felt as if every drop of blood had drained out of her body. She clutched onto the chair in front of her. "Don't say anything more, Barney, please. Don't tell me . . . ."

"I have to, Kate. I have to! She laughed at me! And something just seemed to go off inside of me. Like it did when your dad hit you. All I'd done. All I'd gone through. Just for her." Barney was holding Kate with his eyes now. She couldn't turn away, couldn't even drop her eyes from his.

"Then she laughed again. 'Who do you think you are, you loser?' she said. And I just—hit her. I didn't even remember I had the wrench in my hand. She fell. She didn't move."

"Why didn't you go for help?" Kate made a huge effort to get the words out.

"I tried to pick her up. I didn't know what to do. I thought maybe she was just hurt, but she was dead, Kate. She was dead!"

"How could you know for sure?"

"There was so much blood. She wasn't breathing. You can tell, Kate." He sobbed. Tears streamed down his face. "I looked around. There was nobody there. Nobody had seen what happened. I panicked. I dragged her behind some bushes, then I just took off. When I got home Mom and Dad were out. I had blood on my jacket. Blood on my hands. I washed it all off. . . . I washed the wrench. Even put it back in my tool kit. It's still there." Suddenly he seemed to crumple. Kate let out her breath with a gasp and took a step toward him, but he caught himself and stood, swaying. He made no move to wipe the tears away.

"We've got to call the police, Barney." Kate spoke the words carefully, each one separate from the others.

"No. I can't do that."

"Tell them what you told me. It was an accident. You didn't mean to do it."

"But I killed her. She's not going to come back. She's gone. *I killed her, Kate.*"

Thunder rumbled. Lightning flashed almost immediately. The lights in the snack bar flickered, then steadied. Barney fumbled in his jacket pocket and brought out an envelope. He held it out to Kate. One part of her mind registered the fact that he was holding it in his left hand. Of course. Barney was left-handed too. She'd known that. Known it all along.

"When I heard that guy had come back. . . when I realized he'd be blamed. . . . I didn't like him—hated the way he always hung around you. You were *my* friend. But I couldn't let him be blamed. I wrote it all down. Just like it happened. Just like one of your stories, Kate, except this one's true. You take it. You give it to the police."

Kate reached out for it. Her hand shook wildly, but she moved slowly, deliberately. "We'll take it together, Barn."

"No. For once in my life I'm not going to be stupid. For once in my life I'm going to do the right thing."

Before she could move, he charged over to the door and out. His motorcycle roared.

Kate stared after him, confused, her mind numb with shock. Where could he run to? He'd left his helmet. . . . Then she understood. She tore out the door after him.

"No!" she screamed. The wind ripped the cry away. "Barney, wait!" It was too late. The red taillight blinked away from her into the darkness.

Catch him. Stop him. The keys to the pickup—Angie had them. She'd been using it that afternoon and Kate had seen her drop them in her pocket when she returned. Kate raced for the garage. She hammered at the door.

"Mom!" She felt her knuckles bruise, but she hammered harder. It was only an instant, but it seemed like an eternity before the upstairs window opened and Angie's head appeared.

"Kate, what's happened? What's wrong?"

"It's Barney!" The rain streamed down onto her face. She cupped her hands around her mouth. "Come down, Mom," she shouted. "Bring the keys to the pickup. We've got to go after him."

Angie was down and out the door almost immediately. Kate caught a glimpse of Stacy's pale face in the window, then she ran toward the truck, her mother following close behind.

"Barney was here," Kate gasped as they slid into the cab in a welter of water and Angie shoved the key into the ignition. The pickup started with a cough, and Angie threw it into gear. "He killed Melanie! He told me."

Angie swiveled her head toward Kate; the truck skidded dangerously on the wet gravel.

"*Barney?*"

"Yes. And I'm afraid. . . . I don't know what he's going to do. He's on his motorcycle. We've got to catch up to him!"

Angie swerved out of the station, skidding again as she hit the pavement. She swore under her breath.

The rain was coming down so hard that the windshield blurred after each pass of the wipers. Kate leaned forward, peering into the blackness beyond, willing the taillight of Barney's motorcycle to swim into view.

"Hurry, Mom. Go faster."

"Going as fast as I can." She braked slightly.

"Don't slow down!"

"Have to. Curve's coming up." Angie's voice was clipped, her mouth set.

The yellow warning sign with the curving black arrow that marked the beginning of the bend around the lake flashed past. At the same time a stroke of lightning lit up the road and the woods beside it as if a floodlight had been turned on. It lasted only an instant, but that instant was enough.

"Stop, Mom!" Kate screamed.

Angie braked again, too hard this time. The truck took a sickening lurch toward the shoulder of the road and the trees beyond. Angie fought it back under control and brought it to a stop in a slither of gravel.

"Kate! What—?"

Kate didn't answer. She ripped her door open and almost fell out of it. Heedless of the rain, slipping on the muddy grass underfoot, she ran toward the trees. Shining in the reflected lights of the pickup, a mangled, twisted, red and black motorcycle lay on its side at the foot of a tall oak. Just beyond it, a dark form. Ominously still. Kate fell to her knees beside it.

"No. Oh, Barney. . . . No!"

He had been right. You could tell when somebody was dead. His head was twisted at an impossible angle, and his eyes were open and staring into the rain as if at something only he could see.

Kate sat at one of the tables in the snack bar, methodically shredding a paper napkin.

"I let him down. When he tried to tell me . . . when he needed help . . . I let him down. I called him dumb. I called him stupid."

The storm had passed; early morning sunlight streamed through the windows, and the air was mercifully cool, with almost a touch of autumn about it. Mike, Stacy, and Angie sat with her. The police had come and gone. Mike had returned, cleared of all suspicion. None of them had slept.

"It's not your fault, Kate. How could you possibly have known?" Angie gently took the remnants of the napkin out of Kate's fingers.

"I never really paid any attention to him. He

was just . . . Barney. I was so busy feeling sorry for myself. I never thought about him at all."

"You had a lot to feel sorry for yourself about," Angie answered. "It's been a pretty rotten summer."

"Not as rotten as it was for Barney. I had no idea he felt like that. No idea his parents were that bad. But I should have known—after that day when his father got so mad at him for working here. His father was so unreasonable—almost crazy and he must have just about killed him over that motorcycle. I should have tried to help him. But I didn't." She looked out the window at the empty highway.

"Barney was right about one thing, though, Mom. He was right about Dad. In spite of . . . in spite of everything. He does love us. I know that. I really do. I remember. . . . Remember when he bought me my first bike? He spent a fortune on it, then even washed it and kept it clean for me. He really spoiled me. I know he loved me."

"Still does, Kate," Angie said softly. "He still does. And he's trying so hard."

"Mom?" Kate reached for another napkin, began shredding it. Angie went to take it away, then checked herself.

"When you go to visit him again," Kate went on, "can I go with you?"

"You certainly can," Angie said. She stood up, then reached down to smooth Kate's hair. "He'll be real glad to see you." She straightened her shoulders. "Meantime, I'd better get to work."

Stacy leaped to her feet. "I'll help you."

"You sure you feel up to it?" Angie asked.

Stacy looked at Mike and beamed. "Sure do," she answered. "Got Mike back—I can do anything!" Then she turned serious. "I'm really sorry, Mrs. Halston, for freaking out like that last night. I was just so scared."

Angie smiled and patted her shoulder. "Of course you were. Who wouldn't be? Everything's all right now, though."

"Yes. Thank god." She hesitated for a moment, then turned to Kate. "Whatever I can do—you know? To help?"

"Thanks, Stacy," Kate said. She looked from her over to Mike. The two of them. What a hopeless pair. The odds were so much against them.

But then, who knew? Maybe they'd be the ones to make it. She braced herself for the pain when she let her eyes linger on Mike. Oddly, it wasn't there anymore. Not even when Stacy touched his hand in passing.

"The worms are the worst," Kate called after her.

Stacy looked back and grimaced. "Yeah. I bet." She followed Angie out.

Kate stood up and went over to the window. Mike followed her.

"Kate?"

"Yes?"

"About that knife?"

She stiffened. "Yes?"

"It was an old Swiss Army knife that was rusted shut. I hadn't been able to open it in years. I don't know why I even had it on me."

"Oh, Mike!" The day suddenly seemed brighter. Some of the heavy weight lifted from her. "Why on earth didn't you tell me that?"

He shrugged. "I just got mad. Mad that you didn't trust me. God knows why you should have, but I guess I just got my feelings hurt. Wanted to worry you—hurt you back. Like I said—I'm a jerk."

"You're not a jerk. I should have known better." She turned to look out at the highway again. "So many things I should have known, should have done . . . ." A truck whooshed past, wheels noisy on the still-wet road, then it was empty again.

"Poor Barney," Kate whispered. "Poor Melanie."

Mike laid a hand on her shoulder. It felt comforting.

A few weeks later Kate sat on her stool, resting. It had been a more than usually busy Saturday, and she'd been to see her dad that afternoon. The first time she'd gone it had been awkward, neither one of them had known what to say, but gradually it had gotten better. Today Steve had been full of enthusiasm about the program he was on, full of plans for the future.

"I'm going to lick it this time," he'd said. "I

know it, Kate." His eyes had shone with a gleam she hadn't seen in years. He'd lost weight; his face was no longer pouchy and swollen.

He had reached out, tentatively, to hug her. Instinctively, she had started to draw back, but then, as he clasped her to him, the old, comfortable feeling of safety in his arms—the remembered, beloved from childhood smell of him—suddenly overwhelmed her. She felt tears prick her eyes. She hugged him back. And, for the first time, she allowed herself to hope.

The snack bar was momentarily empty. Summer was over, she was back at school. Mike and Stacy had settled in and were working hard, and Angie—Kate smiled to herself as she thought of her mother. Who would have thought Angie would turn into such a *boss* of a person? She had them all organized and marching around like a well-trained army. The snack bar was positively *humming*!

Kate rested her chin on her hands and stared, unseeing, at the fish tank. Then, almost unconsciously, she reached under the counter for her notebook. Toward the end, when things had gotten really bad, she hadn't been able to write at all. She'd thought she might never write again. Now she picked up her pen.

It was to be a summer of despair, tragedy, and fear, she wrote. *But finally, for some of us, of hope. I didn't know any of this, however, on the morning the boy slammed in through the snack-bar door.*

He looked tired. He looked sick. He was trying very hard to look tough.

The noise from outside didn't bother her. It was the clamor of the old burned-out foundation being torn down, dug up. Mike and Stacy were going to plant apple trees.

"I've got a knife," he said . . . .

About the Author

Karleen Bradford is the winner of the 1992 Canadian Library Association Young Adult Book Award for *There Will Be Wolves*; the 1990 Max and Greta Ebel Award for *Windward Island*; and the Commcept Award for Best Children's Novel for *The Other Elizabeth*. Her many novels for young readers also include *The Nine Days Queen*, *The Haunting at Cliff House*, and *I Wish There Were Unicorns*. A Toronto native, she has lived in England, Germany, the Philippines, Colombia and Puerto Rico. She now lives in Ottawa.

THERE WILL BE WOLVES

Karleen Bradford

Winner of the 1992 Canadian Library Association Young Adult Book Award

"It works its magic with a plot that weaves memorable history lessons into a colourful medieval tapestry of high adventure."

The Ottawa Citizen

The daughter of an apothecary and the owner of a secret book of healing arts, Ursula is determined to become a great healer — but her ambition makes her an outsider in the Holy Roman Empire. When she is accused of witchcraft and sentenced to burn at the stake, she is given one chance to save herself: she must march in the People's Crusade to the holy city of Jerusalem. Along with her father and her friend Bruno, Ursula joins thousands of pilgrims on a harrowing journey, which will expose the dark side of the "glorious" Crusades, and change her life forever.

ISBN 0-00-647938-3
$4.99
mass market paperback

 HarperCollins*PublishersLtd*

THE HUNTER'S MOON
O.R. Melling

Winner of the 1993 Ruth Schwartz Award and Shortlisted for the 1993 Mr. Christie Book Award

"*The Hunter's Moon* is a gripping story. Readers will close the book feeling that they, too, have been on the quest—a sure sign of a successful story."

Quill & Quire

Determined to enter the magical world of Faërie, Findabhair and her Canadian cousin Gwen challenge an ancient law by spending the night in a sacred Sídhe-mound. When Gwen awakens, horrified to discover Findabhair missing, she knows it's the work of the fairy king. Relying on the help of leprechauns, fairy folk and a few red-headed friends, Gwen must use her common sense and her belief in magic to outwit the fairies and rescue Findabhair...before the night of The Hunter's Moon.

ISBN 0-00-64736-7
$5.99
mass market paperback

■ HarperCollins*PublishersLtd*

THE DRUID'S TUNE
O.R. Melling

"...a crackling good story in the tradition of C.S. Lewis."

Quill & Quire

Caught up in the enchantments of Paedre, a modern-day Druid, two teenage visitors to Ireland suddenly find themselves in the midst of an ancient battle. As the companions of the young hero Cuchulainn, they face the invasion of Ulster by the warrior-queen Maeve. Battles commence, danger abounds, then the Druid disappears — leaving Rosemary and Jimmy in the adventure of their lives.

ISBN 0-00-647952-9
$5.99
mass market paperback

HarperCollins*PublishersLtd*

THE LAST WOLF OF IRELAND
Elona Malterre

Winner of a Best Book Award from the American Library Association

"Beautifully written, too good to miss."

Quill & Quire

Devin comes face to face with a great, black she-wolf and all the stories he's ever heard about bloodthirsty animals race through his mind. But the wolf walks away, leaving him with a new respect for these magnificent beasts.

In this legendary and moving tale, a young boy learns to fight against greed, superstition, and ignorance to protect the beauty, intelligence and freedom of the last wolf of Ireland.

"...(an) eloquent, stirring novel..."

Publishers Weekly

ISBN 0-00-647944-8
$5.99
mass market paperback

■ HarperCollins*PublishersLtd*